THE CHICKEN RUN

By the same author

JOHNNY SALTER, *a play*
THE CAR, *a play*
CYCLE SMASH, *a novel*
MARLE, *a novel*

THE RELUCTANT READER

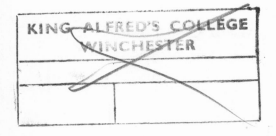

The Chicken Run

A Play For Young People

by

Aidan Chambers

HEINEMANN EDUCATIONAL
BOOKS LTD · LONDON

Heinemann Educational Books Ltd
LONDON EDINBURGH MELBOURNE TORONTO
SINGAPORE JOHANNESBURG AUCKLAND
IBADAN HONG KONG NAIROBI

SBN 435 23167 7

Published by
Heinemann Educational Books Ltd
48 Charles Street, London WIX 8AH
Printed in Great Britain by
Cox & Wyman Ltd.
London, Fakenham and Reading

PRODUCTION NOTES

THE STAGING of *The Chicken Run* must be fluid, speedy and smooth if the play is to be performed successfully. The intention is that each scene shall 'melt' into the next, as in film and T.V. one scene fades into another. On the stage, this can only be achieved if the sets are designed for it, and atmosphere is created by a sensitive use of light.

The bare essentials of each scene are few: a counter and shop chairs for the newsagent's; an armchair and stool for Gran's flat, and so on. If these are designed as trucks, using the kind of universal castors on the market, it is easy to move furniture on and off stage without interrupting the flow of action, and without using a curtain fall. If this movement is matched with the fading in and out of lighting on to each acting area, the effect of one scene melting into another can be effectively created. This requires no great technical ability, but well trained stage and light crews – the kind of work young people enjoy and do well.

In the first production, the climbing ladder used in the playground scenes was kept on stage throughout the play. It was used in other scenes as a device from which set decoration could be hung. Thus in the newsagent's shop, it became an advertisement hoarding; in Gran's flat it became a window merely by hanging curtains from it; and in Slim's bedroom it became a universal headboard from which came Slim's bed and bedside table, and where hung his mirror and a large picture of a speeding motor bike. In fact, the ladder grew in the minds of both players and audience into a very effective and valid symbol of the play's theme.

Despite my worries when writing the play, we encountered no opposition or criticism of the chicken run itself, with its use of candles in a sadistic act, or of the fight with the iron rods. The candle burning is easily staged safely. But the fight with the rods must be for real and is potentially dangerous to the actors, though no more dangerous than sword play on the stage. It is – as always – the modernity of the iron rods which gives the scene such a frightening look. The golden rule is a long, hard-worked period of rehearsal before performance. Accidents only happen on stage when people don't know what they are doing.

As in my other plays, I have avoided giving more than the minimum stage directions so that the imaginations of producers and actors may work freely in the re-creation of the play. Sometimes, as in the smoking scene – 7 – and the shaving scene – 8 – no instruction is given at all except that the incident takes place.

I am always glad to learn what others discovered while producing these plays, and will always help with any points of production referred to me. I can be reached via the publishers.

A.C.

The Chicken Run was first performed by
Archway School, Stroud, on 29th November 1967.

For David Orchard

CHARACTERS

LES PRINGLE, *newsagent*
THE NEWSKIDS:
TROUT
MEGEN
HETTY
ABRAHAM, *a small eleven-year-old*
DAVID JONES, *in charge of the newskids*
SLIM MACKEE, *a fifteen-year-old school leaver*
THE MOBS; *a motor-cycle gang:*
DOBBER, *their leader*
ARCHIE
THE MUTE
THE BIRD, *Dobber's girl*
QUEENIE
WILF
TICH
GRAN JONES, *grandmother to David*
ELSIE MACKEE, *Slim's mother*
WALTER MACKEE, *Slim's father*

The action of the play passes in Les Pringle's newsagent shop, the local playground, Gran Jones' flat, Slim's bedroom, and on a bench by a canal.

It all happens during a Friday evening and Saturday sometime early in May.

ACT ONE

Friday evening

ACT TWO

The following day

ACT ONE

SCENE ONE

LES PRINGLE'S *shop. Five o'clock, Friday evening.* SLIM *is arrogantly lazing.* HETTY *is sorting newspapers.* ABRAHAM *is perched on the counter, while* LES, *next to him, furious, attempts to sort newspapers – a job he long ago delegated to* DAVID JONES. TROUT *is fiddling with a piece of fishing tackle, while* MEGEN *gazes at him.*

LES (*bursting at last*): Not any of you is any use! I might just as well pack in this shop altogether. (*He rubs the small of his back painfully.*) Me back! You're louts, the lot of you.

TROUT: I'm not a lout . . .

MEGEN: That's libel, that is.

TROUT: . . . I'm a teenage rebel.

HETTY: It's slander, Megen, not libel.

ABE: Les . . .

LES: What now?

ABE: I'm not a lout either.

LES: You? You're too young to be a lout. You're just a pest.

HETTY: Oh, Les! Abraham's nice.

SLIM: He's a flippin' pest.

HETTY: You can talk, Slim Mackee! Get your papers sorted.

SLIM: Float off! That Jones kid is supposed to do that.

MEGEN: Slander must be when you *say* something nasty about somebody . . .

LES (*to* ABE): Get off them papers . . .

MEGEN: Libel must be when you write it.

LES: . . . you'll crumple them. (*Wincing again.*) Me back's killin' me!

TROUT: Dave's not here.

LES (*to* ABE): Folk don't want papers you've stood all over.

ABE: Not standing – I'm sitting.

TROUT: Dave's not here.

LES: Sitting's as bad.

ABE: Ain't!

LES: Get off, will you! (*He pushes* ABE *off the counter.*) Blimey – you're enough to drive a saint out of Heaven!

TROUT (*shouting*): Dave's not here.

LES: All right, Trout. All right. So Dave's not here.

SLIM: Well, old Troutie's right. You know, Les – this place just about collapses without that Jones kid.

ABE (*holding up a paper he is reading to show* HETTY): Here, it says here that a kid of fourteen rescued a cat what was caught up a tree. (*Reading.*) 'The boy risked his neck for his four-legged friend,' it says.

SLIM: Enough to make you puke! There's one or two round here ought to risk their necks an' all.

HETTY: Dave rescued Mrs Goldberg's little boy from the canal, but they didn't put that in the papers.

ABE: Not even the local rag, they didn't.

TROUT: Animals is different. They can't take care of themselves.

MEGEN: Neither could Mrs Goldberg's little boy, Trout.

HETTY: And Dave saved him.

LES: You give me the willies, you lot. Dave, Dave, Dave. If Dave ain't here, you're stuck; if Dave ain't here you just sit and wait. Dave's the only one among you with any sense. The whole lot of you is useless!

HETTY, ABE, MEGEN *and* TROUT *shout loud, half-mocking agreements with* LES.

SLIM: Dave's flippin' fan club! Roll on the day I get my machine – you won't see me for dust.

ABE: Nobody will worry.

MEGEN: My mother says motor bikes are the pleasure of fools and God's revenge on the reckless.

ABE (*provocatively*): It'll sure be the pleasure of one fool I know!

SLIM (*menacing*): Watch it, kid!

ABE: Could hardly miss a long string of misery like you!

SLIM: Right – that does it!

SLIM *chases* ABE *round the shop. The others yell after them.* LES, *scarcely containing his irritation, places himself in* ABE'S *path; grabs him as he runs past; and clips his head.* HETTY *comes to* ABE'S *defence, as* LES *holds* SLIM *off.*

HETTY: Leave him alone, Slim. He's smaller than you, and he's only having you on.

SLIM: One day, he'll get what he asks for, the squirt. You're cheeky, kid!

ABE (*none the less cheeky for his clipped head*): Yes, your Lordship!

TROUT: You still after joining them motor-cycle lot – them Mobs?

SLIM: Yeah, I'm joining the Mobs. Why?

TROUT (*withdrawing as he realizes he has attracted* SLIM'S *irritation*): Just wondered, that's all!

MEGEN: You can't join them – you're only fifteen. You haven't got a licence, never mind a motor bike.

SLIM: Time passes – I'll get both. Only eight months now.

ABE: I've heard about them Mobs and their chicken run.

LES: That the lot with the chicken run? Mad, that's what they are. All that chicken stuff. Dunno what their parents is thinking about. Chicken run! Wasn't one of them in the papers?

HETTY: Yes – Archie Mickloe.

TROUT: What'd he do?

MEGEN: Got fined for dangerous driving and had his licence embossed.

HETTY: *Endorsed,* Meg.

MEGEN: Same difference.

SLIM: He was framed. I know him – he's getting me into the Mobs. He was framed – some copper had a down on him.

LES: You believe that sort of guff?

SLIM: Yeah, why?

LES: You ever seen that Mobs lot on the road?

SLIM: Yeah.

LES: Reckless, that's what they are. Don't care for nobody – themselves or nobody.

SLIM (*ironically*): How awful!

LES: Ought to be stopped, they ought.

SLIM: Disgraceful!

TROUT: I heard that during one of them chicken runs, one kid got a broke leg and three fingers smashed.

ABE: Yeah – they was racing towards each other to see who would get scared first and give way.

MEGEN: And what happened?

ABE: They didn't!

MEGEN: My dad would have them all horse-whipped. Horse-whipped he'd have them, and sent to Borstal.

SLIM (*imitating her Welsh accent*): Oo – the charming man!

LES: I'll horse-whip that Dave if he doesn't get here soon. Where is he anyway?

ABE: Goes to his Gran's with her groceries on a Friday.

TROUT: Today's Friday.

SLIM: Bright boy!

MEGEN: You leave Trout alone, misery!

SLIM: What's with you, then? Engaged to him or something?

MEGEN *looks at him, and at* TROUT *and then bursts into tears as she rushes to* HETTY.

TROUT (*puzzled*): What's up with Megen, then?

HETTY (*to Slim*): Now look what you've done. (*She comforts* MEGEN.)

SLIM: So how could I know? (*He's delighted with the effect of his teasing.*)

HETTY (*to* MEGEN): He's only pulling your leg, Megen.

ABE: If we don't start on the rounds soon, we'll miss Moonrocket.

TROUT (*active at once*): Hey – yeah! Moonrocket's on at six.

SLIM (*mocking*): Big thrills!

MEGEN (*still tearful*): Don't know how you get round by six even on normal days. I don't get finished until much later.

ABE: You must dawdle then.

MEGEN: No, I don't. It's all that change – people always give me notes...

SLIM: They see you coming, nit.

LES: Your money was short last week, an' all.

MEGEN: I know, Les. And I'm sorry. Really I am. It's all that change. Never could do sums. I'm trying my best.

ABE: You're trying all right – *very* trying! (*To the others.*) She adds on her fingers.

MEGEN (*furious*): Liar!

ABE: I've seen her.

MEGEN: *Liar!*

ABE: Not!

MEGEN: Are!

ABE: Not!

MEGEN: Are!

ABE: Not!

MEGEN (*beside herself*): Are, are, are. So there!

    Pause.

ABE: *Not!*

    MEGEN *bursts into more tears.*

LES (*exploding at last*): For crying out loud! If Dave doesn't come soon and clear you lot off, I'll go berserk. Where *is* Dave, for Heaven's sake?

    Enter DAVE, *a string bag of groceries over his shoulder. He is an irrepressible extrovert, a naturally popular fourteen-year-old.* HETTY, ABE, TROUT *and* MEGEN *shout their greetings.*

DAVE: Here, for Heaven's sake! Watcher, fans!

SLIM: Oh, God! (*He moves away.*)

DAVE: No need to be formal in the shop, Slim.

SLIM: Mighty mouse himself. The local big-head.

DAVE: Hi, misery. Moping?

SLIM: Get lost.

DAVE: Done your round?

ABE: No, he hasn't done his round. Just sits there.

TROUT: None of us has done our rounds.

ABE: None. Waiting for you.

TROUT: And I wanted to go fishing tonight.

LES: Couldn't start without you. Where's Dave? Where's Dave? All the time – where's Dave . . .

ABE: You was as bad.

LES: Dave ain't here. No peace. All the time, on and on. Get this lot out of here before I go stark, staring, raving bonkers, d'you understand?

DAVE (*mocking*): That's a great speech, Les.

ABE: A great speech. Must have heard it about thirty times tonight.

TROUT (*taken in*): Five times, Abe. Only five times tonight.

ABE: You're deaf.

TROUT: Short-sighted, that's why I wear specs.

ABE: Thought they was to keep your ears apart.

TROUT: Didn't have them 'till I was eight.

ABE (*in mock amazement*): Didn't have ears 'till he was eight!

TROUT: No! Didn't have specs 'till I was eight!

HETTY (*packing her papers into a newsbag*): My papers are ready. I'm off.

LES: Thank goodness somebody is off.

SLIM: She's been off for years.

LES: For mercy's sake, Dave. Get them on the road. If you hadn't been so late, they'd have been finished by now.

DAVE: Got held up.

SLIM (*mocking*): With Granny's groceries?

DAVE: With Grumbler.

ABE: Grumbler Grind?

DAVE: Grumbler Grind.

HETTY: Why did he keep you in, Dave?

DAVE: Combing.

ABE: Your hair?

DAVE: My hair.

MEGEN: Not worth combing your hair.

TROUT: Where, Dave?

DAVE: In his Geography lesson.

ABE: You'd be for it, then. He hates people combing their hair.

MEGEN: That's because he hasn't got any himself. Not any.

HETTY: He has some round the edges, Megen – it's cute.

ABE: Yeah – like a grass verge.

HETTY: What did Grumbler say, Dave?

> DAVE *has been sorting the papers into newsbags and distributing them. He pauses, assumes a mock school-teacher attitude, takes* ABE *by the shoulder and does an act, mimicking his conversation with Grumbler.*

DAVE: He said, 'Boy!' he said. 'Boy, what do you think you are doing, eh? Doing, eh? Eh?'

ABE: So what did you say, Dave?

DAVE: So I says . . . (*He drops to one knee and pleads.*) 'Oh, nothing, sir. Nothing.' (*He stands, the schoolmaster again.*) 'That's very strange, Jones,' he says. 'I could have sworn you were doing your hair, lad.' (*He curls his fingers in* ABE'S *hair until he has a handful.*)

ABE: So what happened, Dave?

DAVE: Grumbler looks for a minute, see, then he says . . . (*His head is bent down level with* ABE'S, *and he repeats Grumbler's words in one breath.*) 'The Education Authority of this town does not spend two hundred pounds a year on your education so that you may carry out your private toilet either upon their premises or during times when more academic studies are intended to be pursued.'

ABE (*amazed*): Crikey, Dave, how come you remember all that guff?

DAVE: Simple, Abraham. Grumbler made me write it out fifty times.

LES: Look, Dave, for the last time – it's quarter-past five, and nobody has moved an inch with them papers, and that blower will start ringing any minute now and there'll be customers yelling at me, wanting to know what's gone wrong with their papers. Besides which, it's collecting night. (*He winces.*) Me back! Get this lot going, before there'll be more than lines to write out. There'll be wages stopped.

TROUT (*galvanized again*): Say no more – money talks louder than words. (*He grabs his newsbag.*) See yer at the playground in an hour, Dave.

Exit TROUT.

DAVE: Now don't blow your top, Les. It only makes your back worse. Come on everybody.

MEGEN: Oo – now for it! All them notes! All that change!

Exit MEGEN.

DAVE: O.K., Hetty?

HETTY: Yes, thanks.

DAVE: Got ours, Abe?

ABE: All here, Dave. I've put Gran's groceries in the bag.

SLIM (*taking his papers*): Like a flippin' pantomime this place.

DAVE: Look, Slim – get going, will you?

SLIM: Keep your shirt on, kid. Think you was the Prime Minister.

DAVE (*trying to draw* SLIM *into a joke*): Careful, Slim. Les votes for that lot.

LES: What's that? That I do. Why? Who's taking the Prime's name in vain?

SLIM: Ah – Belt up!
        Exit SLIM.

LES: Somebody is going to take that lad down a peg one day.

DAVE: Bit shirty, isn't he?

ABE: He stinks, Les. Stinks.

HETTY: It's not all his fault. I wouldn't like to live at his house myself.

ABE: His mum's O.K. A bit wet. But his dad stinks. Worse than Slim, his dad is.

DAVE: Come on, Tadpole, let's go. We'll call at Gran's on the way round.

SCENE TWO

A Street. DAVE *and* ABRAHAM *are on their round.*

ABE: Dave?

DAVE: Yeah?

ABE: When am I going to have a round of my own?

DAVE (*stopping and confronting* ABE): Sick of me, are you?

ABE: No, Dave, it's not that. You know it isn't that. Just want a round of my own.

DAVE: You're not ready yet – haven't been at it long enough. You'd be worse than Megen with the change.

ABE: I wouldn't, Dave. Honest. I haven't made a mug of the money for three whole weeks.

DAVE: True.

ABE: Not for three whole weeks. I just want a round of my own with my own customers and all that.

DAVE: I know how it is, Abe. I was just the same when I started. I went round with Les. Three years ago that was – and he wouldn't let me have a round of my own for six months.

ABE: Six months! What for?

DAVE: Les believed in proving yourself – proving you was properly interested in something before you took it on yourself.

ABE: He's not like that now. He let Slim Mackee on without making him go round with anybody at all.

DAVE: It's his trouble with his back has done that. He hasn't been the same since last winter when he caught that sky-attica.

ABE: Bad tempered with it an' all.

DAVE: Believed in proving yourself, Les did. But I'll talk to him about having a round of your own. Next week maybe.

ABE: Thanks, Dave. It's not that I don't want to be with you – it's just I want one of my own, that's all.

DAVE: I know, Abe, and you shall. I'll talk to Les next week – didn't I say I would?

ABE: Thanks, Dave.

DAVE *is about to push* ABE *on ahead of him, when he looks, off, as though at the house ahead. An idea comes to him, and he grins.*

DAVE: Look – here's a chance to prove yourself. Les will want some proof, you know. (ABE *begins to realize what is coming and struggles with* DAVE.) Deliver Dancy's papers. You needn't collect the money.

ABE: No, Dave! Not Dancy's! Anything but not that!

DAVE: You'll be O.K.

ABE: No, Dave – any other house, but not this one. That dog of theirs. It's mad. Even Les doesn't like going in there.

DAVE: So? You might get a house like this on your round. You'll have to go in then. Thought you was ready for a round of your own? (*He holds the papers out.*)

ABE: I am, Dave, but . . . (*He steels himself and snatches the papers.*) Well . . . all right . . . But if I get chewed to death, I shan't take the blame.

DAVE: Away you go.

ABE *turns, approaches the wing, cautiously, and with trepidation. He looks back at* DAVE.

ABE (*heavily ironic*): Well – so long . . . *friend*!

As though going to his death, ABE *exits. As soon as he is off stage, a vicious growl is heard, which, accompanied by yells from* ABE, *grows in viciousness until we hear what sounds like an attack.*

ABE *reappears, as though having jumped a garden gate, falls in front of* DAVE, *who has been enjoying the sight, and springs up at once, his hands clasped behind him, covering his behind.*

DAVE: You did it!

ABE: It was nothing!

DAVE: Great. That's the proof Les will want. Great!

ABE: Nothin' at all. Anybody could have done it.

DAVE (*beginning to wonder about* ABE'S *stance, with his hands behind him*): You O.K.?

ABE: Eh? Oh – yeah!

DAVE (*edging round to see, but* ABE *edging too, so that his back is visible to the audience*): What's with the hands then?

ABE: My hands? They're all right. (*He holds his hands in front of* DAVE'S *face.* ABE'S *trousers are ripped open and his shirt is hanging through the gap.*)

DAVE: Oh. Thought you must have hurt them.

ABE: No. My hands are fine. (*He puts his hands behind him again.*)

DAVE: Well, that was great, Abe. You'll get your round, you'll see. Now – come on. We've got to call at Gran's.

> DAVE *pushes* ABE *ahead of him. Once on their way,* ABE *takes his hands away from the seat of his trousers.* DAVE *sees the damage at last, and has a private laugh.* ABE *walks on painfully.*

SCENE THREE

GRAN JONES' *flat. An armchair and footstool.* GRAN *has fallen asleep over her knitting.*
As they approach, DAVE *stops* ABE *in his tracks.*

DAVE: Now go steady – Mum says Gran's heart is as dicky as a broken old clock spring.

ABE: Will she die soon, Dave?

DAVE: Cheerful Charlie, you are!

ABE: I don't want her to die, Dave. I just meant . . .

DAVE: I know what you meant. She ain't going to die yet
'cos we ain't going to let her. So come on, and be
quiet. She might be sleeping.

    DAVE *and* ABE *approach* GRAN's *chair cautiously.*

DAVE: You awake, Gran?

ABE: Awake, Mrs Jones?

GRAN (*waking and smiling when she realizes who they are*):
Hello, boys.

DAVE: We got the groceries, Gran.

ABE: In the bag, we got them.

GRAN: Good lads. Put them on the stool. Ta, love.
Lovely. Even got me Complan, an' all. Ain't they just
two angels! Put them out back, Dave.

    DAVE *exits with the groceries.*

ABE: Mrs Jones – Dave's going to talk to Les about me
having a round of me own.

GRAN: He is? Good. Time you was prompted.

    Enter DAVE.

DAVE: *Promoted*, Gran.

GRAN: You're late today?

ABE: Dave was kept in.

GRAN: Kept in!

DAVE: Mr Grind. I was combing my hair, you see.

GRAN (*amused*): Combing your hair! You lads! You
ain't a hair-comber usually, son. Not usually, are you?

ABE: He's been combing all over the place lately, Mrs
Jones. I seen him during lessons last week, when I was
passing his classroom, and there he was – combing.
Bound to be caught sometime, wasn't he?

GRAN: Growing pains, that's what 'tis. Growing pains.

His dad was just the same. He was a bit older when it happened to him, but happen it did. Right tearaway he was at sixteen: combs and clothes, and then to top it all – girls. Girls it was with your dad, and that's next on your list, I've no doubt.

DAVE: Get off it, Gran!

GRAN: You'll see. Same with your dad, and look at him now.

DAVE: He still likes them!

GRAN: When they're all topless dresses and bottomless skirts he does, likes them all right then. None so sure he even notices your mother.

ABE: Girls is a waste of time.

GRAN: There's folk wouldn't agree with you there, Abraham.

ABE: Well then, they're daft. My brother Benny – he went and got a girl, and he rues the day. (*Imitating a sour-voiced Benny.*) 'I rue the day I got married to *that*,' he says now. Well I ain't gonna rue that day. I'm gonna stick to my airyplanes.

GRAN (*laughing*): Very wise, Abraham.

DAVE: You're nuts, Abe. Gran, Mum says you ain't to go traipsin' about doing cleaning. She says she's coming in next Monday to go through the flat for you.

GRAN: The day your mother has to clean my flat is the day they carry me out in my coffin.

DAVE: Well – that's what she said.

GRAN: Very nice too, I'm sure. But if I can't look after myself, I don't want anybody else to be bothered, thanks. I'd rather go on to where your Grandad's gone. Unless they've sent him down you-know-where, and I don't know I'm so keen to join him there.

ABE (*scandalized*): Do you think they have, Mrs Jones?

GRAN: What, son?

ABE: Sent him down . . . you-know-where?

GRAN (*chuckling*): Shouldn't be at all surprised. Not after the life he led before I married him. He was all for the drink and the women.

DAVE: He was all right after you got him though, Gran.

GRAN: That he was, David. And many's the time he used to say that if the Lord sent him to Hell, he'd be very surprised.

ABE: Why, Mrs Jones?

GRAN: Because, Abraham, Mr Jones always said that I'd given him Hell on Earth, that's why.

DAVE: Honest, Gran, you're nutty.

GRAN: When you're seventy-three so will you be, so less cheek, I say.

DAVE: Well, there ain't no such thing as the Devil. It's like Santa Claus really.

ABE: How do you mean, Dave, it's like Santa Claus?

DAVE: Well – it is, isn't it. The Devil is like Santa Claus. It's your dad really.

ABE: You try telling my dad that!

DAVE: Or mine!

GRAN: Get along with you, you daft happeth!

DAVE: We are, Gran. But we'll be back.

GRAN: Aye – with the money.

DAVE: Yeah – and because of it being your birthday.

GRAN: Oh! Am I to have presents then!

DAVE: You never know!

GRAN: Oo – I say!

SCENE FOUR

A bench by a canal. MEGEN *is sitting trying to sort her rounds money. She is depressed.*

Enter HETTY.

HETTY: Hi, Meg. How you doing?

MEGEN (*delighted to see a friend*): Oh, Hetty, I'm in an awful tangle, I really am. I've given Mrs Hooper too much change, and Mr Carter too little, and I'm all of six bob down with folk I can't remember. It's awful, Hetty.

HETTY: However do you manage it?

MEGEN: It's all them notes, you see, and folk stand at their doors with the television blaring and they want to get back to see, and well, I get all hot and bothered, and then it happens, you see. What'll Dave say, Hetty?

HETTY: It's not what Dave'll say that matters, Meg. It's Les that's to be worried over.

MEGEN: But Dave takes the money first, at the playground he takes it, and he'll want to know about my losses.

HETTY: Never mind, Meg. I don't expect he'll eat you.

MEGEN (*looking down the road and grinning suddenly*): I don't mind being eaten – not by some I could mention! (*Worried again.*) It's having the losses taken out of my wages that bothers me. It's my transistor, you see.

HETTY: How do you mean – it's your transistor?

MEGEN: Well, you see, my dad bought me a transistor on the H.P. and he said that I could have it so long as I give him the money regular every week. Any week I miss and the transistor goes back, he says. Back to the shop. Well, I was down last week, and he let me off. But he won't let me off two weeks, not my dad, and I can't do without my transistor, Hetty.

HETTY: I'll have a talk to Dave. He's bound to be able to do something.

MEGEN: Oh, thank you, Hetty. You're a gem! I just knew you'd help. Hope you don't mind.

HETTY (*playing the lady a little*): Don't mind talking to Dave about anything, so it's no bother.

MEGEN (*taking up the hint with enthusiasm and curiosity*): You like him then?

HETTY (*responding with more assumed sophistication*): He's improving with age.

MEGEN (*innocently*): Can't say I've noticed, myself.

HETTY (*reaching the heights of superiority*): But then, you haven't my . . . experience, Megen!

MEGEN: No, that's true, I'm glad to say.

HETTY (*angered*): Megen Bliss, that's a nasty remark.

MEGEN: It just slipped out, Hetty. I didn't mean . . .

HETTY: I've a jolly good mind not to say anything to Dave about your losses for that.

MEGEN: Don't say that, Hetty – think about my transistor. I'd be lost without it, I really would. (*She looks along the road again and is agitated at once.*) Oo – look! Trout's coming. His streets and mine meet here.

HETTY: O-ho! Now I see why you're always so late – it's not the money at all!

MEGEN: It is, Hetty. Honest it is.

HETTY: You sit here like patience on a monument waiting for Trout.

MEGEN: No I don't – well – not for long. Usually he doesn't even notice me.

HETTY: Honestly, Meg – you're hopeless!

MEGEN: Shush, he'll hear you. Look, do me a favour, Hetty. Just slip off and leave me alone.

HETTY: Wouldn't dream of coming between you and a conquest! See you, Meg – be careful with the small change!

Exit HETTY.

MEGEN *settles herself in what she hopes is a fetching position on the bench, just in time.*

Enter TROUT, *puffed.* MEGEN *coughs exaggeratedly.*

TROUT: Watcher, Meg. Didn't see you thera. Rushing to get finished.

MEGEN (*with heightened tones of a maiden in distress*): Oh, Trout. I haven't finished either. Isn't it terrible?

TROUT: Awful. I feel as bad about it as you do.

MEGEN: You do?

TROUT: Something ought to be done about it – like a strike or something.

MEGEN (*simpering*): Oh, Trout!

TROUT: I think I'll tell him about it.

MEGEN: Thank you, Trout.

TROUT: I'm missing it too.

MEGEN: You're missing it too?

TROUT: Yeah – same as you!

MEGEN: Trout . . . ?

TROUT: Yeah?

MEGEN: What are you talking about?

TROUT: Moonrocket. It started at six and it's ten-past now.

MEGEN (*stamping her foot and pouting at her disappointment*): Oh, Trout. I was talking about my money!

TROUT: Your money! You haven't gone and messed it up again?

MEGEN: Yes . . . and I thought . . . well . . . you're so good about money . . .

TROUT (*pleased*): I am?

MEGEN: And so intelligent . . .

TROUT (*suspicious*): Eh?

MEGEN: And so strong . . .

TROUT: Megen . . . ?

MEGEN: And so *terrific* with Les . . .

TROUT: Meg . . . are you sure you haven't mixed me up with somebody else?

MEGEN (*rubbing against him*): Silly! (TROUT *gets hot under the collar.*) I'm talking about you. I thought maybe because you're so intelligent . . . and strong . . . and . . . and *courageous* . . . (*They are almost off the end of the bench.*) you might try to help me. (MEGEN'S *hand comes over* TROUT'S *shoulder.*)

TROUT (*swallowing hard*): Help you! How? I . . . I ain't got any spare money, if that's what you're after.

MEGEN: It's not your money I want, Trout.

TROUT (*feeling things are getting worse*): It isn't? . . . What then?

MEGEN (*joining her hands round his neck*): Just . . . help.

TROUT: Well . . . I could put in a word for you with Dave.

MEGEN: Hetty is already going to do that.

TROUT: She is? That's O.K. then, isn't it?

MEGEN: I need *support*. (*Her leg suddenly puts a lock on him, so that she is almost sitting on him.*) *Masculine* support.

TROUT (*drowning*): Masculine support?

MEGEN: Uh-huh. I need to *belong* to somebody.

TROUT (*with all his dying strength, standing up*): Well, sorry, Meg – I've got my rounds to finish.

TROUT *dives away up the road, shaking* MEGEN *from him as he goes.* MEGEN *sprawls on the ground.*

MEGEN (*thwarted*): Oh . . . BOYS!

SCENE FIVE

The local playground.

The essentials in the scene are a playground climbing ladder and a collection of old boxes of various sizes, which children have been playing on, and which when sat on by someone as big as Dobber seem to suggest a throne.

There is a roar of approaching motor bikes, which grows almost deafening before they stop and cut out just outside the playground.

Enter DOBBER *with* BIRD, ARCHIE, MUTE, QUEENIE, WILF *and* TICH. *They are dressed, apart from Bird who is in the latest gear, in black leathers, riding boots, and crash helmets. Their faces are almost entirely covered in scarves worn over their mouths and noses, and these scarves seem to be the only individual distinguishing marks, for each one is a different colour.* DOBBER'S *is white,* ARCHIE'S *yellow,* MUTE'S *red,* QUEENIE'S *green,* WILF'S *blue, and* TICH'S *black. They enter with assumed coolness and nonchalance, and yet something about them suggests barely*

*held, violent energy. They seem unordered, and yet their
stances and grouping and the very way they move leaves
one wondering whether all these have not been carefully
studied.*

*They are looking about them as they enter, and finally turn
in their studied disorder, to take in the playground from
another angle. We see for the first time that each one has
on his back, in white, the outline of a coffin, standing on
end. The coffin makes a body with a grinning skull for
head, wings for arms, and bones for feet. Inside the coffin
are set the letters:*

M

O B

S

DOBBER *sits on a box, and the others group about,* WILF
*climbing the ladder as a lookout. As they move, they take
off their helmets, pull down their scarves, and open their
leather jackets. We see them for the first time as individual
people. All are at least seventeen, look hardened and quick
to act rather than talk. From the moment he speaks, it is
clear that* DOBBER *controls them.*

DOBBER: So where's the kid then, Archie?

ARCHIE: How should I know where he is? I told him,
here, on the playground soon as you've finished your
round on Friday, I told him. How should I know
where he is?

QUEENIE: Forget it, Dobber. Let's go. I'm bored – want
some action.

ARCHIE: Women! Look, Queenie, dear – the kid'll
come.

QUEENIE: Sucks!

DOBBER: What's his name?

ARCHIE: Slim.

DOBBER: Slim what?

ARCHIE: How should I know what his name is? Slim – ain't that enough?

WILF: Could be any kid.

DOBBER: You mean you didn't ask him . . . ?

TICH: Could be any kid out for a giggle.

DOBBER: . . . I told you before . . .

MUTE: It's Mackee.

ARCHIE: The Mute speaks.

DOBBER (*shouting them down*): . . . Always find out about new kids.

MUTE: It's Mackee. The kid's name's Mackee – I've seen him about. He was in the first year when I left school. He's wet, Mackee.

BIRD: Then I hope he doesn't talk Scottish, Dobs, because I can't bear people who talk Scotch.

DOBBER: Archie won't be talking to anybody soon. (*He jabs* ARCHIE *in the stomach with his boot, knocking him backwards.*) Always check – nig-nog!

ARCHIE: O.K. O.K. The kid's all right. I know him.

DOBBER: And you don't know his name? Who's he muck with?

ARCHIE: He doesn't muck with anybody – he's the usual type. Wants a bike more than he wants to live.

MUTE (*ironically*): We know the feeling!

QUEENIE: Idiot!

DOBBER: And he thinks being in the Mobs will be all wide open throttles and skid-pads, eh?

ARCHIE (*sourly*): He thinks it'll be all fun and games. So that's one thing he'll get a shock about!

C

DOBBER *comes at* ARCHIE *almost before the words are out of his mouth, and grabs him by the scarf, manhandling him harshly.*

DOBBER: You want to stay in the Mobs, eh? Then drop the bright remarks – O.K.?

ARCHIE (*struggling and in pain*): O.K. – it was only a joke.

DOBBER: It's the sort of joke I don't like, see. This ain't no Sunday school outing, boyo. So toe the line – O.K.?

ARCHIE: It was only a joke, I tell you.

DOBBER: Hard to get in – easy to get out. (*He pulls* ARCHIE'S *head to one side and then smashes it to the other side, lifting his knee to collide with it as he does so, before thrusting* ARCHIE *away.*) Right?

The OTHERS: Right!

DOBBER (*still yelling at* ARCHIE): You want to be out? (ARCHIE *shakes his head, which he is massaging painfully.*) Then toe the line, or it won't be just the chicken run for you, mate. (*He returns and sits on the box again. Quietly, but still with menace*): Now, let's try it again. Who's the kid muck with?

ARCHIE: He's in that newspaper set. Les Pringle's kids.

MUTE: What – the one that Jones' slob runs? That one?

ARCHIE: Yeah.

QUEENIE: Oh, Dobber. That kid's still in his nappies. Archie's kidnapping. That Slim can't be more than fifteen.

ARCHIE: So what – Granma! He's keen and he wants to be in – we could use a kid like that.

MUTE (*provocatively*): What for, Archie? Cleaning your machine?

ARCHIE (*going to* MUTE *and squaring up to him*): Look, Mute, stick to your name and keep your trap shut.

MUTE: Or?

ARCHIE: You'll have some swollen lips to seal it up.

DOBBER: Shut up. Archie's got the kid to come, so we might as well look at him.

QUEENIE: So where is he?

ARCHIE: I'll go and find him.

Exit ARCHIE.

QUEENIE: For Heaven's sake, Dobs, keep kids out.

DOBBER: Look, Queenie – we need new kids. There ain't nothing wrong in it. It's good to have kids coming on – new blood and all that.

MUTE: I never knew Archie do anything that didn't have something in it for him. But – kids come and kids go. One day – us too. The Mobs has got to keep going so we need new kids.

DOBBER: Long live the Mute. That's the longest speech I ever heard you spout. I don't care if these kids are still driving their prams, let's have them when they're keen.

QUEENIE: There'll be trouble.

DOBBER: What fun!

QUEENIE: But there's no point in asking for trouble, is there?

DOBBER: You must be ageing, Queenie! Who asks for trouble? Have we ever done anything the coppers have nicked us for? The record's clean, girl: we've always done things that way and always will. Oh – a bit of speeding here and there maybe, but what's that between friends?

QUEENIE: There's the chicken run. That's hardly legal.

DOBBER: So we do some tough things during the run. O.K. What's it to the law? It's us together, everybody agreeing – yeah? It doesn't ever bother anybody but us, does it? So what's it to the law?   They do worse flippin' things in the army than we do in the run, so who's to care? The kid'll be all right – I'll see to that.

WILF: Is it the usual routine when the kid comes, Dobber?

TICH: A glare-in, first?

DOBBER: Yeah – the usual. But look – lay-off a bit with him so young.

MUTE: Let him have it same as usual, I say.

DOBBER: You heard, Mutie. Play it cool.

Enter SLIM *with* ARCHIE *following.* ARCHIE *pushes him into the middle.*

ARCHIE: He was waiting at the gate.

BIRD (*singing coquettishly*): 'There was I, waiting at the gate . . .'

ARCHIE: He thought we'd be in the road.

SLIM (*defensive*): The bikes were there.

DOBBER: And we're here. O.K. – let's do a glare-in.

The MOBS *settle in various places about the playground, surrounding* SLIM, *and stare at him. There is not a sound or a movement.* SLIM *becomes, as the seconds pass, more unnerved. He glances round at each person; he makes a silent appeal to* ARCHIE, *who doesn't bat an eye-lid. He looks at* DOBBER.

SLIM: Look, I . . .

DOBBER: Just pipe down.

The glare-in continues. Finally, completely unnerved, SLIM *backs for an exit, but when he turns to run he finds the massive* TICH *blocking his way. He turns back and makes for* DOBBER, *his temper beginning to rise at the treatment.*

SLIM: Look – what's the . . . ?

MUTE (*shouting him down*): Shurrup!

> SLIM *stands for a moment and at last folds his arms,
> breathing heavily with frustrated irritation. The glare-in
> goes on a second or two longer.*

DOBBER (*quietly*): He's a bit fragile by the looks of him.

TICH: The kid's weak.

WILF: Couldn't take a long drink of water.

QUEENIE: You want to be in the Mobs, kid?

SLIM: Yeah.

MUTE: For?

SLIM: I like motor bikes.

DOBBER: So you want to be in the Mobs?

SLIM: Yeah.

DOBBER: It ain't just motor bikes with us, kid. This is a
sort of clan – you know?

SLIM: I know what it's like.

WILF: There's others.

SLIM: There ain't a kid in town wouldn't prefer the
Mobs to the others.

DOBBER: That's the style, youngun. That's cos we run
proper, see? This ain't no sloppy lot. We run stricter
than an army.

MUTE: I don't think he has what it takes.

ARCHIE: Look – I tell you he's got bags of spirit.

MUTE (*spoiling for some action*): Has he? Let's see.

DOBBER: Easy, Mute.

> MUTE *crosses to* SLIM, *who squares to him, anticipating
> trouble.* MUTE, *grinning, looks him up and down before
> suddenly and violently knocking* SLIM *against the climbing
> ladder. Recovering,* SLIM *lunges at* MUTE, *who side-steps,
> avoiding* SLIM'S *attack.* SLIM *tries a number of moves but*

MUTE, *still grinning, and completely relaxed, avoids them all in an adept but tantalizing manner.* SLIM *at last is tripped by* MUTE, *and falls at* DOBBER'S *feet. Before he can stand up,* DOBBER *pushes him down again with his foot.*

DOBBER: O.K., kid – cool off. Mute was only teasing.
>DOBBER *kicks* SLIM *away.* SLIM *stands up slowly, brushing himself down, and angered rather than subdued by what has happened.*

SLIM: Then he's got a funny idea about teasing.

DOBBER: He's a funny bloke. You'll learn. Sit down.
>SLIM *sits on the box next to* DOBBER.

DOBBER: Now – a few questions.
>DOBBER *waves the others to him. They gather round the box,* QUEENIE *leaning closely on* SLIM'S *shoulder.*

DOBBER: What you work at Les Pringle's for?

SLIM: Money.

DOBBER: What's the money for?

SLIM: To buy a bike.

MUTE: How old?

SLIM: Fifteen and two months. I leave school this term, thank God.

MUTE: How much you saved?

QUEENIE: Enough for a top class machine?

SLIM: Enough for a two-fifty.

ARCHIE (*almost as an aside*): Have you now?

DOBBER: You got to have a good bike, or that's your lot.

TICH: Even Queenie's got one.

QUEENIE (*slinkily*): And I'm a girl!

SLIM (*looking her up and down*): Nobody would have guessed!

QUEENIE (*recoiling and slapping his head*): Don't be cheeky.

ARCHIE: Who said he didn't have what it takes!

QUEENIE: Ah – nuts! (*She goes to the ladder and sits on it.*)

MUTE: The Bird hasn't a machine.

DOBBER: A special case, ain't yer! (*He kisses her.*) You'll have a bike. (*To* SLIM.) Next point. The chicken run.

WILF: You heard of that, kid?

SLIM: Yeah – I've heard of it.

WILF: It's a sort of test, see? If you can stand the run, you can stand anything.

TICH: Then you're in.

MUTE: You want to do a run?

SLIM: Yeah.

QUEENIE: Think him up a run, Dobber.

ARCHIE: He can't do it on a machine – he's too young.

DOBBER: You're right for once. So we got to think up something else.

WILF: Something juicy.

BIRD: That one you gave that other kid . . .

DOBBER: That Matlock kid?

BIRD: . . . turned my stomach. Give this one something less messy.

DOBBER (*pondering a moment*): O.K. See yer, kid. (*He gathers* BIRD *to him as he passes her, shouting back to* SLIM *as he goes.*) Here, tomorrow morning, for the chicken run. Nine o'clock. And don't be late!

Exit the MOBS. *As they go,* HETTY *enters the opposite direction and watches them go, standing by the ladder. There is a roar of starting motor bike engines, which then speed away.*

SLIM *is sitting on the boxes, his back to* HETTY, *whom*

he has not seen enter. As the noise of the motor bikes roar off, he takes a cigarette from his pocket and lights it.

HETTY: That was that Dobber and the Mobs, wasn't it?

SLIM (*looking round at her*): Yeah – why?

HETTY: You trying to get in, are you?

SLIM: What's it to you?

HETTY: Nothing – just asking.

SLIM: So I'm trying to get in. Shall, too.

HETTY: Wouldn't touch them with a barge pole personally.

SLIM: That's a laugh! With the Mobs it's whether they'd touch you.

HETTY: Maybe. (*Pause.*) Why do you want to join them?

SLIM: Look – lay off, will you? I want to join them – the rest's my business.

HETTY: Just interests me, that's all. I wouldn't want to belong to a set like that.

SLIM: Who wants to go kicking round with a bunch like your newspaper lot? I mean – look at them. That Trout kid for a start. Like a wet leek in a cabbage patch. And that Megen – a Welsh face flannel dripping soapy tears for the Trout. The Jones' kid ain't much better. His head is about as big as you can get without bursting. As for that Abraham – that little kid! He just makes me want to puke. Who'd want to be like that – eh? I want to belong to something worthwhile – you know? Something that's going places. (*Sourly.*) And there ain't many of those.

HETTY: So you chose the Mobs?

SLIM: Nobody chooses the Mobs. They choose you. You know, there ain't a kid in town doesn't want to belong to the Mobs. Oh, they don't say so. They even say the Mobs stink. But underneath they're dying to be in. They haven't the nerve to try it, see? They're just scared of the chicken run, or what their dads will say.

HETTY: That's better than not caring at all.

SLIM: Is it?

HETTY: Don't you care what your parents say?

SLIM: Look – my dad might be walking around, but as far as I'm concerned he dropped dead years ago.

HETTY: That's not a very nice thing to say about your dad.

SLIM: My dad is not a very nice man.

HETTY: Anyway, you're too young to ride yet.

SLIM: When I can, you won't see me for exhaust.

HETTY: I think you're a fool.

SLIM: The feeling's mutual.

Enter TROUT, *running.*

TROUT: Keep her off me, Het!

HETTY: Keep who off you?

TROUT: That Welsh witch – she's after me.

SLIM: What's up, Troutie? The Welsh passion on the flood?

TROUT: She's gone funny, Het! (*He yells as he sees* MEGEN *and runs on to the boxes behind* HETTY.)

Enter MEGEN, *running, and excited.* HETTY *holds her off from chasing* TROUT *further.*

MEGEN: Trout! What you run for?

TROUT: I'd my round to finish.

HETTY: Leave him alone, Meg.

SLIM: Let her catch you, Trout – have done with it.

Enter DAVE *and* ABRAHAM, *briskly.*

TROUT (*relieved they have arrived and excited by his news*):
I did it again, Abe – knocked two minutes off my
round today.

ABE: How long now?

TROUT: Forty-eight minutes.

ABE: However do you manage it?

SLIM: He was being chased by a Welsh trog.

MEGEN: Watch your words, bacon-rind.

ABE: You go on cutting minutes off like that and you'll
end up meeting yourself before you start.

DAVE (*businesslike*): Look – come on – money.

SLIM: Seven pounds eight. O.K. (*He puts the money on
the box.*)

DAVE (*checking his list and putting the money into a money
bag*): Right. Trout?

TROUT: The usual – eight-pounds-three. I counted it
four times between the *Crown and Anchor* and here.

ABE: And you still beat your record?

TROUT: Yeah – counted it in my pocket as I came. Four
times I counted it.

ABE: You said. Don't know how you do it.

HETTY: He had Megen behind him.

ABE *and* TROUT *go to a corner, talking between themselves.*

DAVE: No wonder he went fast! How much, Megen?

HETTY: Megen has a problem, Dave.

DAVE: So has Trout by the sound of things.

HETTY: She's six bob short.

MEGEN: It's the change, Dave. I got mixed.

DAVE: Not again! Look – I've told you before: if you
must be wrong, at least have too much and not too
little. You'll have to have it stopped out of your wages.

MEGEN (*beginning to be tearful*): Oh, no, Dave. Not that.
I'll make it up somehow, but don't stop it out of my
wages. It's my transistor, you see?

DAVE: No, I don't see.

MEGEN: Tell him, Hetty, won't you? When he gets
annoyed I go all of a dither.

HETTY: If her wages are stopped her dad will send her
transistor back to the shop. Can't you do something,
Dave?

DAVE: Then you should always be more careful with
the change. It's always the same – always wrong
change. She ought to be sacked.

   MEGEN *bursts into sobs;* HETTY *comforts her.*

HETTY: She's getting better, Dave: it was eight bob
last week – it's only six this. Maybe somebody could
go round with her, to get her confidence back.

DAVE: O.K. One more try. After that – out. Trout.

TROUT (*breaking away from talking with* ABE): Yeah?

DAVE: Next week you go round with Megen and do
both your rounds together.

TROUT: What – Megen and me?

ABE: Atta-boy, Trout!

HETTY: Dave! Honest!

MEGEN (*recovering and looking at* TROUT *with delight and
anticipation*): Oo – thanks, Dave. You're a gem. There's
this week's six-pounds-four. That's six bob short. I'll
make it up somehow – and I wouldn't want anyone
but Trout to go around with. (*She is advancing on him,
and* TROUT *is backing away.*)

TROUT: I think I'd rather not, Dave.

DAVE: Your money, Het.

HETTY: Nine-pounds-two-and-six.

DAVE: Spot on, thanks. You got Gran's present?

HETTY: In my paperbag. Taking it now, are we?

DAVE: Yeah.

TROUT (*desperately, having been driven into a corner by* MEGEN *who is trying clumsily to fondle him*): It'll finish me, Dave.

DAVE: With our round, that makes forty-two pounds and sixpence. We're there, bar Megen's six bob.

SLIM (*who has watched the collection carefully*): You leave that with your Gran?

DAVE: Yeah. Going there now. It's her birthday an' all.

SLIM: Never did know why you leave it there.

HETTY: It's nearer the playground than Les's shop, and Les is closed by the time we've finished collecting on a Friday. We've always done it.

ABE: Pick it up in the morning.

SLIM: I see. (*Making for the exit.*) Crummy idea!

ABE: You think of something better then, *genius*!

SLIM (*stopping and menacing him*): Watch it, kid.

ABE: Ah – go gas yourself in an exhaust pipe.

SLIM: Ah – go drown yourself in a puddle.

   Exit SLIM.

   TROUT *breaks from* MEGEN.

TROUT: Dave . . .

DAVE: Yeah?

TROUT: Call her off, Dave.

   TROUT *scrambles up the ladder and stands on top.* MEGEN *climbs half-way up to him.*

HETTY: You oughtn't to chase him in public, Meg.

MEGEN: I only wanted to make arrangements about next week.

TROUT: There ain't no arrangements to make, *witch*!

ABE (*shouting from the top of the boxes*): Careful, Trout, she might turn you into a maggot.

MEGEN: I just want to show you my list.

TROUT: I don't want to see your list. I want to go fishing.

HETTY: Come on, Trout – be brave. She won't eat you.

ABE: She will if she turns him into a maggot.

TROUT: Lay off, will you!

ABE (*singing raucously*): 'Nobody loves me . . .'

DAVE: Come down, Trout.

ABE: '. . . everybody hates me . . .'

MEGEN: I only want to talk to him.

ABE: 'I'm going to the garden to eat worms'!

TROUT: Yeah – about masculine support – I know!

DAVE (*delighted*): Is *that* what she talks to you about! Masculine support! (*He and* ABE *are creased with laughter.*)

TROUT: Well, I ain't comin' down.

MEGEN: Then I'm coming up.

> MEGEN *starts to climb to* TROUT. *In desperation,* TROUT *opens his newsbag, upside down, rams it over her head and jumps from the ladder.* MEGEN, *the bag over her head, falls.*

HETTY: Careful, Meg.

DAVE (*as* MEGEN *falls*): Grab her!

TROUT (*as he exits*): I'm going fishing – by myself!

> *Exit* TROUT.

MEGEN (*struggling up*): Trout! Trout! Wait for me. Oo-aren't boys difficult! Trout!

> *Exit* MEGEN.

> DAVE, HETTY, *and* ABE *collect their things.*

DAVE: Poor old Trout. He's had it now.

ABE: Girls stink!

HETTY: Abe! I thought I had a friend in you!

ABE: Girls stink – except you!

HETTY: Thanks, Abe.

DAVE: Come on, let's get over to Gran's. She'll think we've forgotten her. Bet she nearly dies when she sees that hat.

ABE: Yeah – loves hats, your Gran does.

SCENE SIX

GRAN JONES' *flat.*

GRAN *is knitting as she hears their approach, she pretends to sleep. There is much hushing, giggles and whispers from* DAVE, HETTY *and* ABRAHAM *before they come in. They surround* GRAN'S *chair, walking on tip-toe.* DAVE *beats 'one . . . two . . . three' and they burst into a raucous, near-tuneless version of Happy Birthday.* GRAN *protects her ears.*

GRAN: What a noise! You scared the life out of me – thought the end of the world had come.

DAVE: Get on, you old fraud – you weren't asleep.

ABE: Hetty's got something.

HETTY (*putting a parcel on* GRAN'S *lap*): For you from Dave, Abe and me. (*She kisses* GRAN.) Happy birthday, Gran.

DAVE and ABE: Happy birthday.

GRAN: A present! Well I never! Haven't had presents for years. You get past the age, you know. And then all of a sudden people start giving you them again. I reckon I've got that far.

DAVE: Adam was your dad, wasn't he, Gran!

GRAN: Cheek! (*Pulling a hat from the parcel.*) Oo – look at that! A hat! Now how did you guess I'd like a hat!

HETTY, DAVE and ABE: I wonder!

ABE: Put it on, Mrs Jones.

GRAN: But I'm not dressed for it!

DAVE: Course you are.

HETTY: Please put it on, Gran.

 GRAN gets up and puts on the hat.

ABE: Looks like a lamp-shade! Where's the light switch!

 ABE and DAVE collapse into laughter.

HETTY: Abe! That's not nice. It looks lovely, Gran.

GRAN: Does it, Hetty? Will I look all right in the street?

DAVE: Lovely. Far better. Nobody will be able to see your face!

GRAN: You're a cheeky young brat, Davie Jones. There's just one thing, Hetty.

HETTY: What's that, Gran?

GRAN: Well, this afternoon, I had a trip out. (*She takes a parcel from behind her chair.*)

DAVE: You haven't been traipsing again, Gran?

GRAN: Hold your mouth, big ears. I'm talking to a lady.

ABE: That's no lady, that's Hetty!

HETTY: You wait.

ABE (*holding rounded fingers to his eyes*): You can't hit a man with glasses.

DAVE: Ladies and gentlemen, pray silence for her majesty, Granny Jones.

GRAN: You lot – you'll be the death of me!

DAVE: Come on, Gran. What did you go traipsing for?

GRAN: Well, as a matter of fact, I went out this afternoon and saw something I just couldn't resist . . .

DAVE: Gran, you haven't . . .

HETTY: Not a . . .

ABE: What, Mrs Jones . . . ?

GRAN: I got this.

   GRAN *produces a hat – it is an exotic creation, a folly of a hat.*

HETTY, DAVE and ABE: A new hat!

GRAN: Just couldn't help myself.

DAVE: You ought to be under an armed guard. (*He snatches it from* GRAN.) What is it anyhow?

   HETTY *tries to take it from him,* ABE *causes confusion.* DAVID *escapes.*

DAVE: What is it, Gran? A greengrocer's shop?

   They laugh. He throws the hat to ABE *and signals for silence.* DAVE *does a jumbled, breathless dance routine, singing* EASTER BONNET, *and making* GRAN *and* HETTY *join in.* ABE, *wearing the creation, conducts and sings from the footstool.*

GRAN: Stop it, for Heaven's sake.

   ABE *runs to* DAVE *with the hat and returns to the stool, which he places upstage of* GRAN'S *chair, and stands on.*

ABE: Go on, Dave, show the hat off. Be like one of them fashion models – all neck and legs and no bust or backside.

HETTY: Abe!

   DAVE *takes the hat to a corner, back to the room. When he turns round, the hat completely covers his face, and he is standing like a glossy magazine model.* ABE *holds an imaginary microphone to his mouth and mimics the speech of a fashion commentator. As he speaks* DAVE *minces round the room, displaying the creation.*

ABE (*mimicking*): And here we have our latest style in headwear. Ladies and gentlemen, the Greengrocer style. Newly devised by the house of Jones, and worn here by our charming model, Belinda Breezeblock. The hat is reasonably priced at a hundred guineas. The model costs a little more.

GRAN: I shall have heart-failure if this goes on!

DAVE (*throwing the hat into her lap*): Get on with you – you're as fit as an ox.

HETTY: It's time we went anyway, Gran. See you to-morrow.

GRAN: Right-o, dear. Thanks for the nice present. I shall walk in the park tomorrow, and wear it if it's a fine day. And I don't know when I've laughed so much.

DAVE: Here's the paper money, Gran. (*He takes the money bag out of his newsbag.*) Forty-two pounds and sixpence. Don't go and blue it all on a binge tonight. Where shall I put it?

GRAN: Put it in the hat box, then we'll both remember where it is. I'm getting that forgetful.

DAVE: I'll not forget, I can tell you.

The money is put in the hat box and placed on the stool.

GRAN: Well, you just come in the morning and get it, son. If I'm in bed, I shall know who it is, and that saves you from bothering me. Good night, Davie.

DAVE: Night, Gran.

ABE: Night, Mrs Jones. Mind the bugs don't bite!

GRAN: Goodnight, Abraham.

Exit DAVE, HETTY and ABRAHAM.

GRAN *looks at the hat, stands, comes down stage, looking out into the audience as though into a mirror. She tries*

*the hat on, and looks at herself, before she chuckles at
herself.*

GRAN (*to herself*): Silly old woman!

    Exit GRAN.

SCENE SEVEN

*The playground. Late that night. There is a hint of street-
lamps.* ARCHIE *is lying on the boxes, and* SLIM *is sitting
beside him, smoking.*

SLIM: What'll Dobber give me for a run, Archie? You
    know – I mean exactly?

ARCHIE: Now that would be telling, mate.

SLIM: You know, do you?

ARCHIE (*raising himself up on to his elbow*): We've just
    decided, kid. All of us together. And yours is easy –
    honest. Easiest run we've thought up yet. (*With the air
    of the person in touch with those who matter.*) 'Well,' I
    says to Dobber, 'that kid, Slim, he's O.K. Tough as
    old Nick.' And so Dobber says to me, 'Right, Archie.
    You say so – he's O.K. We'll give him an easy one.'
    You'll walk it, kid.

SLIM: There ain't nothing I want more than my own
    bike and to ride with the Mobs.

ARCHIE: You'll get in the Mobs all right. Leave it to
    me, kid. And if you can afford a bike when the time
    comes, you're made.

SLIM: I'll be able to afford it.

ARCHIE (*sitting up, face to face with* SLIM): You loaded
    then?

SLIM: Got a fair bit.

ARCHIE: Dunno where you get it all from.

SLIM: That paper round for a start.

ARCHIE: What, that two-bit thing! Tell us another and I might buy it.

SLIM: Honest – look – whatever I make on the round I stash away. Then there's an odd job here and there, and me Sunday morning round. And at the end of this rotten term I leave the prison-camp . . .

ARCHIE: What a tearful day that will be!

SLIM: I dunno how I live through it! Well, then I'll get a job, and the money I save from that – well – there'll be enough for a machine by the time I'm ready for a licence.

ARCHIE: What about the essentials of life then?

SLIM: How do you mean?

ARCHIE (*ironically*): Sweet innocence! The birds, mate, and the fags. Skint me between them. Don't leave enough to keep my machine on the road.

SLIM: Easy. The birds – wouldn't touch them. The fags? For them, I touch my old mum!

They laugh.

ARCHIE: This Jones kid – what's his line?

SLIM: How d'you mean?

ARCHIE: Well – it's common sense, ain't it? He's not running them newskids for fun. I mean, what's he do with the money you said he collects here on a Friday night?

SLIM: Takes it to his Gran's.

ARCHIE: What – that old boot that lives across the road? Her?

SLIM: Yeah.

ARCHIE: What's he do that for?

SLIM: Says he leaves it there 'till morning, then takes it to the shop.

ARCHIE: Bet he fiddles the books at his Gran's. Told you there was a line somewhere.

    Enter ABRAHAM.

ABE: Oh – look what the cat left behind!

SLIM: Watcher, Tich! Off home to bed, are you?

ABE: What's it to you?

ARCHIE: Late for little boys to be out alone.

ABE: Like me to change your nappies for you, then?

ARCHIE (*to* SLIM): O-ho! Frying tonight! (*To* ABE.) Join the party, kid.

ABE: What party?

ARCHIE: We're celebrating Slim's last night as a snotty-nosed schoolboy. Tomorrow, he joins the Mobs.

ABE: Slim does?

SLIM: Slim does!

ARCHIE (*holding out a packet of cigarettes*): Have a fag, kid.

ABE: Don't smoke. You're daft.

ARCHIE: Ah, come on! Don't be snooty. Join the happy throng. You won't stop Slim now.

SLIM: Too right he won't.

ARCHIE: So you might as well join in the celebrating. Live – have fun. Mummy ain't looking, and I promise not to tell. Go on – try one.

ABE: Well . . . maybe . . . just one, just for a try.

    ABE *takes a cigarette which he holds ineptly.*

ARCHIE: That's the style, youngun. (*He lights the match, but* ABRAHAM'S *ineptitude blows it out.*) Suck, don't blow, dope! (*He lights another match.*)

There follows a pastiche of a boy smoking for the first time. Plainly he does not like it, but he perseveres, puffing great clouds of smoke into the air. The other two are delighted at their success.

SLIM: Cor! Call out the flippin' fire brigade.

ARCHIE: Where's that bucket of water, Slim?

SLIM: Good job he's not in a smokeless zone, eh?

ABE'S puffing goes on.

SLIM: Just been dumping the takings, have you?

ABE (*between puffs*): Yeah!

ARCHIE: Must be quite a haul each week?

ABE: Forty-two quid.

ARCHIE: Forty-two quid! Maybe I ought to take up a news round!

ABE is beginning to look sick, and is puffing with less and less enthusiasm. The other two look closely at him.

SLIM: Here, Archie – he's looking green round the gills.

ARCHIE: What's up, kid – don't you like the brand?

ABE is near nausea. He takes one last determined puff.

ABE: It's great . . . great . . .

ABE lays the cigarette on the boxes and with sudden urgency rushes to the wing, where he is sick. We see his rear poking out from the proscenium arch, and at last his creased face. The two on the boxes are delighted by the effectiveness of the jape.

ABE: I think I'll be off now.

ABE staggers away and exits.

ARCHIE: Here, hang on, kid. You haven't said goodbye!

ARCHIE and SLIM laugh. ARCHIE stands up from the boxes.

ARCHIE: I'm off to the shack. Coming?

SLIM: Yeah. (*He picks up* ARCHIE'S *yellow scarf from the box.*) Hey, you've dropped your scarf.

ARCHIE: Thanks. Always losing that damned thing.

Exit ARCHIE *and* SLIM. *There is the roar of a single motor bike engine. The machine goes off up the road.*

END OF ACT ONE

ACT TWO

SCENE ONE

SLIM'S *bedroom. Saturday morning.*

An alarm clock rings, and is thumped out by SLIM *who is covered by the bedclothes. A pause before* MRS MACKEE'S *voice calls, off.*

MRS MACKEE (*off*): Slim! (*Pause.*) Slim! (*Pause.*) Slim, love, it's 7.30. Your alarm's gone.
    SLIM *stirs in the bed.*
MRS MACKEE (*off*): Slim – come on, pet. You'll be late for your round.
SLIM (*muttering*): So what!
    Pause.
MRS MACKEE (*off*): D'you hear? Your dad will be in there in a minute.
SLIM (*to himself*): Fat lot of difference that will make.
    MRS MACKEE *enters. She is in her dressing gown, and sloppy slippers: her hair is in curlers. She carries a cup of tea in one hand and* SLIM'S *shoes in the other. While she talks she slops round the room, picking up* SLIM'S *strewn clothes, and tidying.*
MRS MACKEE: I've brought you some tea, son. Now get up, there's a good lad. You know how you go on if you're late for your round and you always are on a

Saturday. Your dad'll be in if he hears you aren't getting up and you know what it'll be then.

SLIM (*still under the clothes*): Yeah – a lot of hot air.

MRS MACKEE: Your breakfast will be ready by the time you're up and dressed. I've cleaned your shoes all ready for you. (*She sits on the side of the bed.*)

  SLIM *pushes himself up to a sitting position.*

MRS MACKEE (*leaning over and fondling him*): How's my bonny lad today then?

SLIM (*pushing her away*): For crying out loud, Ma! Quit it, will you! Slobbering on. You're worse than when I was a kid. Flip off while I get dressed.

MRS MACKEE (*rising and addressing the room*): He's getting modest in his old age. You'd think his own mother hadn't seen him before.

SLIM: Look – I'm passing the mothering age, can't you see that?

MRS MACKEE: I was only being nice, Slim.

MACKEE (*off*): Is he up?

MRS MACKEE: There you are – you've set your dad off now.

SLIM: A bomb would set him off best. (*Yelling.*) Yeah – he's up.

MACKEE (*off*): Lord flippin' Muck! I suppose he's had his tea?

MRS MACKEE (*going*): All right, all right, yours is coming – jealous guts.

  Exit MRS MACKEE.

MACKEE (*off*): Not so much of the jealous guts, neither. Just remember where the money comes from in this house.

  SLIM *gets up and dresses sourly. He is tired and bad–*

tempered. He drinks the tea as though it were medicine, and at last, sits on his bed, yawns, scratches, and rubs his face. He discovers his face is rough with an embryo beard. It is the first time he has noticed it. He smiles to himself, and feels about his face. He goes to a mirror and looks at the 'growth', delighted with himself. An idea comes to him, and he exits. There follows a three cornered conversation shouted about the house.

MACKEE (*off*): And don't spend all flamin' day in that lavatory.

SLIM (*off*): I'm not going to the lavatory.

MACKEE (*off*): Then don't spend all flamin' day in that bathroom.

MRS MACKEE (*off*): He'll not be long, Walter.

MACKEE (*off*): That kid has first and best use of everything. I'll be home one day and find the house sold above me head.

SLIM (*off*): That's a laugh – it ain't worth selling.

MACKEE (*off*): You're sharp enough about using it like a hotel anyroad. You want to get out of it if you think like that.

SLIM (*off*): I shall – soon enough.

MACKEE (*off*): Nobody will mourn yer!

MRS MACKEE (*off*): I shall. I shall mourn him – won't I, love?

MACKEE (*off*): You! You'd mourn if the cat lost its kittens.

Enter SLIM, *carrying a shaving bowl, razor, brush and towel. He pulls a chair to the bedside, and puts the shaving gear on it. He takes a hand mirror and leans it against the chair back. He sits on the end of the bed and prepares to shave. There follows a pastiche of a boy performing his first shave. While he has been preparing, the voices of his mother and father have gone on off stage.*

MRS MACKEE (*off*): It's time you were up an' all, Walter.

MACKEE (*off*): Hold your noise, woman. I haven't finished me first fag yet.

MRS MACKEE (*off*): Then your breakfast can go cold, for I shan't keep it hot. I'm ready now.

MACKEE (*off*): You might be. I'm not.

MRS MACKEE (*off*): You'll die in that bed if you're not careful.

MACKEE (*off*): Happen it's the best place to die, anyroad, so there's no worry there.

SLIM *manages to shave most of his face, pleased by the effect of his effort, when enter* MRS MACKEE.

MRS MACKEE (*calling to Mackee*): Ee – look at our lad! He's shaving.

SLIM (*taken by surprise*): Look – why can't you knock before you come in!

Enter MACKEE, *in vest and trousers, which he is just finishing pulling on. He is a hard-bitten, sour-looking man, growing flabby from self-indulgence.*

MACKEE: What's he doing? (*He goes to* SLIM *and looks closely at him treating him deliberately with superior patronage.*) So he flamin' is! (*Chuckling.*) Why don't you put some milk on your face and let the cat lick it off? (*He finds his own joke funny, but stops short when he sees the shaving gear.*) Here – is that my shaving gear? Well I'm damned! Who the Hell said you could use that flamin' stuff?

SLIM (*bristling too*): Nobody said I could use that *flamin'* stuff.

MACKEE: Just you mind your language in this house, you spineless oaf.

SLIM: You're not so much cop yourself.

MRS MACKEE: Now don't start arguing, you two.

MACKEE: Hold your mouth, woman. I'm talking to Lord Muck, here. I'm just about fed-up with his high-handed manners and his big ideas. You're growing too big for your boots, me lad, and it's time you was brought down a peg or two.

SLIM (*disdainfully*): By who?

MACKEE (*rising*): By me – that's who!

SLIM: You and who's army?

MACKEE (*real anger threatening*): Will you listen to him! You're not so big I can't give you a leathering, so don't push your luck. You're not as thick as a thick chip when all's said and done.

SLIM: Better than looking like a bloated cabbage, like you.

MRS MACKEE: It'll end in tears.

MACKEE (*boiling*): They'll be his, not mine.

SLIM (*with real venom*): Ah – belt up!

MACKEE (*exploding*): That's done it . . . !

MACKEE *grabs* SLIM *and there is a struggle.* MRS MAC-KEE *tries to part them.*

SLIM: Let me go . . .

MRS MACKEE: Stop it, the pair of you.

MACKEE: . . . you've gone too far this time . . .

SLIM: . . . I'm warning you . . .

MACKEE: . . . I'll show you who's boss here . . .

MRS MACKEE: Walter! Slim! (*Forcing herself between them.*) Stop it, will you!

They part, leaving MRS MACKEE *exhausted between*

them. The struggle has solved nothing and the argument simmers on.

MACKEE (*breathing hard*): Spineless, that's what he is. Like all his age.

SLIM: Here we go again . . .

MACKEE: When I was his age I'd been working two years.

SLIM: . . . My Life and Hard Times, shot three hundred, take one!

MACKEE: We respected our parents, didn't speak to them the way he speaks to us. Been a clout round the ear comin' if we had.

SLIM: Say on, Macduff.

MACKEE: All he's good for is doing a newspaper round and slobbering over motor bikes. Motor bikes! Toys, that's what!

MRS MACKEE: Do give up, Walter.

MACKEE: Fought a world war, I have.

SLIM: Lord knows how we won.

MACKEE: Slaved to keep my home and family together and well provided for. Has he ever lacked for anything? Has he ever been denied anything? Hasn't he always had the best of everything? Eh? And who's provided it? Just tell me that. Who?

MRS MACKEE: Do give up . . .

MACKEE: Me . . .

MRS MACKEE: . . . Walter.

MACKEE: . . . that's who. But does he appreciate it? Do I get any thanks? Has there ever been a minute when he thought about returning some of it? Never! Not one. He might as well be a flippin' stranger, some kid I've never even seen before.

SLIM (*shouting*): I am!

MRS MACKEE (*startled*): Slim!

MACKEE (*stopped in his tracks*): What's that?

SLIM (*moved to the pit of his being*): I am. That's what.
I *am* a stranger. You never have seen this *kid* before.
Just tell me when we last met. Go on. I don't mean
come across each other – not that. But *met*. You know
– said anything that meant something. Or did anything together just because you're my dad and I'm
your son. God! It's embarrassing to talk about it like
that. Like talking about being sick! But go on – tell
me. The last time you did anything for me was when
you pushed my pram up the street. And I wouldn't
bet you did that more often than you need.

MACKEE (*after a shocked silence*): Do you hear him, Elsie?
Eh? He's off his rocker!

SLIM: I'm off my rocker! (*He glares at his father a moment
then snatches up the hand mirror which he holds in front
of Mackee's face.*) Just try looking at yourself, dad.
Because that's the face I see every day of the week.
And when I look at it, I know one thing; nothing –
but nothing – is going to make me like that!

MRS MACKEE: Slim!

MACKEE (*beginning to tremble with rage*): So – it's insults
now, is it?

SLIM: Not insults – just a game of telling truths for once.

MRS MACKEE: There's no need to be nasty to your dad
though, Slim.

SLIM: *Me* not be nasty! What about him? It's all right
for him to spill his rotten insides out, is it? But not
for me to speak my mind.

MACKEE: You're not old enough to get a job, me lad,

never mind speak your flippin' mind. Get some age behind you first.

SLIM: For crying out loud, dad – what's all that got to do with it? You know, dad – you can't see past the end of your own nose.

MACKEE (*beyond his patience at last*): Did you ever hear anything like it, Elsie? I'll tell you something, boy. There's going to be some changes round here. You'll toe the line in this house. We'll have some discipline for a change. For one thing – you'll stop coming in so late . . .

MRS MACKEE: It was near twelve last night, son.

MACKEE: . . . and for another, you'll chuck that motor bike lot you've been sucking up to lately. Don't think I haven't seen you.

MRS MACKEE: They're no good, Slim.

SLIM: How do you know what they're like?

MACKEE: You'll stop seeing them, you understand?

SLIM: I'll not.

MACKEE: You will, and that's flat.

SLIM: I'll not . . .

MACKEE: . . . set of lay-abouts . . .

MRS MACKEE: Dangerous they are . . .

SLIM: . . . and I'll get a bike, an' all . . .

MACKEE: . . . lazy, spineless parasites . . .

MRS MACKEE: . . . that chicken run! . . .

SLIM: . . . I don't care what you say . . .

MACKEE: . . . never done a day's work in their lives . . .

SLIM: . . . I'm doing more than seeing them . . .

MRS MACKEE: . . . don't know what the police are thinking about . . .

SLIM: I'm joining them.

MACKEE: . . . only good for . . . (*He stops short.*) You're *what?*

SLIM: I said, I'm joining them.

MACKEE: Joining who?

SLIM: The Mobs.

MACKEE: You're flamin' well not.

SLIM: I am. *Today.*

MRS MACKEE: No, Slim!

MACKEE: You're right there, Elsie. No he is not.

SLIM: I am, so you needn't try and stop me.

MRS MACKEE: I don't know where he gets it from.

SLIM: You wouldn't!

MACKEE (*exasperated with disgust and rage*): Fancy wanting to belong to a bunch like that! Isn't it good enough for you to belong to the human race?

SLIM (*equally full of rage and disgust, and glaring back almost nose to nose with his father*): NO! Not with you in it!

 There is a pause as the two glare at each other, before MACKEE'S *final words rise from his stomach like the outraged bellow of a wounded animal.*

MACKEE: Why you nasty-minded, Pop-age pipsqueak!

 MACKEE *hits* SLIM *hard across the face, and sends the boy sprawling over the bed.* MRS MACKEE *gasps impotently, her sympathies dividing her.* SLIM *gets up slowly and confronts his father again, as though offering himself for another blow.* MACKEE *expires like a leaking balloon.* SLIM *walks past him, gathering his coat as he goes, and exits without looking back.* MACKEE *turns as* SLIM *goes by, watching his son. As* SLIM *exits,* MACKEE *sits slowly on the end of the bed.* MRS MACKEE *sits at his side, but unable to touch her husband. The scene fades out.*

SCENE TWO

LES PRINGLE'S *shop.* MEGEN *is sitting on the counter.*
HETTY *is standing behind the counter: they are talking*
together. LES *is brushing the floor.*

MEGEN: I just can't get anywhere, Hetty.

HETTY: Trout isn't exactly the best person to choose,
Meg. Why not try somebody else?

MEGEN: What, and be beaten by Trout? Never! I'm
determined now. Maybe, I should write him a
romantic letter?

LES: Maybe you should do some romantic work, young
lady – like sorting them papers.

MEGEN: Oh, Les! This is important. If I fail with Trout
I might never succeed in love again!

LES: And if you fail with them papers, you might not
succeed in keeping your job.

HETTY: But this is important, Les. I know just how she
feels.

MEGEN: Out of all your experience, Hetty, what do you
think I should do?

LES: Out of all her *what*?

MEGEN: Oh, shut up, Les. Men never understand these
things. To men, the heart is a closed book.

HETTY: Come over here, Meg. (*They move away from
the counter.*) Never mind Les – he's only teasing.

MEGEN: Now, Hetty. How do I catch Trout?

HETTY: Same way as he catches fish, I suppose.

MEGEN: How do you mean?

HETTY: Well, you see, there are three ways of catching most men.

MEGEN: *Three!* Nothing is simple!

HETTY: Shut-up, and listen. First of all, you've to look right. That's to catch their eye. When you've caught their eye, you've got to . . . well . . . *interest* them.

MEGEN: However do you do that, Hetty?

HETTY: You are a problem, aren't you? Well, the best way is by pretending that you're interested in the sort of things they do. And with some men, that takes some doing! Remember, there's nothing a man likes more than feeling he's just the most fascinating person alive – the great babies!

MEGEN: And what's the third bit, Het?

HETTY: Well, that's just as the saying says: The quickest way to a man's heart is through his stomach.

MEGEN: That sounds an awful painful way of doing things.

HETTY: For some men, it is, Megen.

MEGEN: My mum's a marvellous cook.

HETTY: Then that explains how she keeps your dad, because I can't say she's much of a picture to look at. Now. Let's start with point one.

MEGEN: That's about looking right.

HETTY: You're learning fast. Let's have a look at you.
   MEGEN *stands, and displays herself. Like her mother, she is no picture.*

HETTY: Yes! Well, there's things to be done there!

MEGEN: But, Hetty – Trout doesn't even notice me.

LES: That I can understand!

HETTY: Hush, Les. Well, maybe there's something we can do about Trout's interests.

MEGEN: His fishing?

HETTY: From now on, Megen, you have a craze for fishing.

MEGEN: I do?

HETTY: You do!

MEGEN: But I hate it, Hetty – all them wriggling white maggots Trout has, and them poor fish. I couldn't bear seeing one of them caught on one of Trout's horrible hooks. I should faint, I just know I would.

HETTY: Do you want Trout?

MEGEN: Yes, but . . .

HETTY: Then get into training to like fishing. When is he going again?

MEGEN: Soon as he's finished his round this morning. He always goes after his round on a Saturday morning.

HETTY: Then you are going too.

MEGEN: I am?

HETTY: You are. I'll see to that.

MEGEN: What do I do when I get there – cook?

HETTY: Whatever for?

MEGEN: Well, Hetty, if the quickest way to a man's heart is through his stomach, then I might as well get Trout on that one as soon as I can.

HETTY: Honestly, Meg – you're hopeless. But maybe you've a point there. What does Trout like most to eat?

MEGEN: Easy – Maltesers.

HETTY (*to* LES): Les, half-a-pound of Maltesers, please, and can we borrow your bad weather things? You don't use them now you aren't out on rounds.

LES (*passing her the sweets*): What for?

HETTY: Megen. She'll take care of them, and it's just for today.

LES: Ain't bad weather today.

HETTY: Please, Les, don't be awkward – you'll see in a minute.

LES: Anything to keep the peace. They're out the back.

Enter ABRAHAM.

ABE: Hi, Het!

HETTY: Hi, Abe. Dave hasn't come yet, and I'm operating on Megen.

ABE: Can I help – there's things I'd like to do!

HETTY (*pushing him out*): Then go out back and fetch Les's bad weather things.

ABE: What for?

HETTY: Get them and you'll see.

Exit ABRAHAM.

LES: You know, this place is more like a flippin' booteek than anything. When am I expected to get any work done?

HETTY: We won't be long, Les.

Enter ABRAHAM, *carrying yellow P.V.C. coat and sou'wester.*

ABE: Is this what you want?

HETTY: That's them. Now, come here, Megen.

They dress Megen in the waterproofs.

HETTY (*standing back*): There – if Trout doesn't notice you in these, he never will. Lovely!

Enter TROUT, *carrying his fishing gear.*

TROUT (*rushing in but stopping short and gazing at the sight of Megen*): I've finished my round, Les. O.K.?

LES: Thank goodness somebody has. See yer tonight.

HETTY: Hi, Trout . . . going fishing?

TROUT (*still gazing at Megen*): Hi, Het. Yeah. Good day for it too.

MEGEN: Hi, Trout!

TROUT: Expecting rain, Meg?

MEGEN: No – silly!

TROUT: Goin' to the seaside, then?

MEGEN: Honestly, Trout, I'm going fishing.

TROUT: Good . . . ! Going fishing?

MEGEN: Why not?

TROUT: No reason at all. In fact . . . every reason why you should. Great sport. Only . . . well . . . I didn't know you liked fishing.

MEGEN: I can't bear . . . (HETTY *coughs.*) . . . think of anything I like more.

TROUT: That so? (*He looks a moment longer, then turns away.*) Well – have a good day.

MEGEN: But, Trout!

HETTY (*stopping him*): Megen was hoping you might take her along with you.

TROUT: What for?

HETTY: Well . . . she's not very good yet and she thought . . . . she thought you might give her a few hints.

ABE (*to* LES): I could give her a few hints – like why don't she go and drown herself!

TROUT: Well, I dunno. (*He considers a moment.*) So long as she doesn't get in the way.

    MEGEN *produces the sweets and holds them out.*

MEGEN: Have a Malteser, Trout.

TROUT: Thanks. You got many of those?

MEGEN: Might have. Half-a-pound I think I bought.

TROUT: You did? Let's see. (*He takes the sweets.*) If you're coming with me, I'd better keep these for you – just in case they get wet.

ABE (*to* LES): He's a sharp kid, you know!

TROUT: And as you're learning, maybe you'd better carry this gear.

ABE (*to* LES): Very sharp!

MEGEN: What – all that!

TROUT: That ain't much. And learners always carry the gear.

MEGEN: Well this learner . . . !

HETTY: Megen! Remember.

MEGEN: Oh – all right. Come on.

    She grabs up the gear, takes TROUT'S *hand and pulls him out with a jerk. Exit* MEGEN *and* TROUT.

LES: Like a flippin' music-hall. Where's Dave? He's late again this morning.

ABE: He's always late on Saturday mornings. Starts late and goes to his Gran's for the money.

    Enter DAVE, *rushing, puffed, and worried.*

DAVE: Abe, Abe!

ABE: What's matter?

DAVE: Have you been to Gran's this morning?

ABE: No, why?

DAVE: Have you, Het?

HETTY: No, why, what's the matter?

DAVE: Plenty by the look of it.

ABE: Well, *what?*

DAVE: The money's gone.

ABE: What money?

HETTY: Not the . . . ?

LES: You mean . . . ?

DAVE: Yeah! The paper money. The week's takings.

HETTY: It can't have done, Dave.

DAVE: I tell you it has. We've searched everywhere. Had Gran's flat upside down.

ABE: It was put in the hat box.

DAVE: I know. But Gran thinks she took it out and left it lying around last night. She's awful worried.

HETTY: Poor Gran.

LES: How much? Ought to have been about 43 quid.

DAVE: Forty-two pounds and sixpence.

LES: I've told you before about leaving it at your Gran's. Asking for trouble. Told you before – you should bring it straight back here. Lazy it was, that's all. You just couldn't be bothered.

DAVE: It wasn't that at all. It was done to save bothering you after you've closed. You're always on about folk who come after hours.

HETTY: For Heaven's sake, stop arguing, it gets us nowhere.

LES: I'm telling you – you find that money by dinner time or it's a police job. And if they don't find it, then you'll all chip in to make it up. Stop your wages, that's what I'll do. Forty-two quid is a deal of money and it's not made as easy as it's lost. So get cracking and do something about it.

ABE: It wasn't Dave's fault, Les . . .

LES: And you can shut your trap, you hear? Unless you got something sensible to say. I'm fed up of your stupid cracks.

HETTY: That isn't fair, Les, taking it out on Abe.

LES: You an' all, missie. You and Dave is as thick as thieves. Now I wash my hands of it.

DAVE: What you going on for? I haven't got that money. Is that what you're saying? I wish I had – save all this bother.

LES: I know nowt about that. All I know is, I'm forty-two quid down and that you was responsible for it. I've always said, once you get taken on here, you're responsible for your own money, haven't I?

DAVE: Yeah.

LES: Right. And then things get slacker and slacker until something like this happens. So you can brace up.

DAVE: All right – so it's my pigeon.

LES: It is that. So think on. You've got 'till dinner time, then it's the police.

There is a dull silence. Exit LES.

DAVE: What I don't understand is who took it. Nobody, not an ordinary burglar, would go into Gran's. They're all old people's flats. They'd know there would be nothing worth pinching.

ABE: Maybe Trout or Megen collected it.

HETTY: I went round with Megen today, just to help her out. And Trout's too keen to go fishing to bother about the money. He'd have said, anyhow.

DAVE: Slim wouldn't have gone for it, would he?

ABE: Wouldn't lift a finger to do more than he's paid for, he wouldn't.

HETTY: He's been in already, anyway, to tell Les he would be doing his round later.

DAVE: What – in before me on a Saturday? His mother can never get him up on Saturdays. What does he want to do his round later for? (*Calling.*) Les?

LES (*off*): Well?

DAVE: What time did Slim come in today?

LES (*off*): Was here soon after I opened – about 8.0 o'clock.

DAVE: Never!

HETTY: I think I know why he was early, Dave.

DAVE: Why?

HETTY: He's doing the chicken run with the Mobs today.

DAVE: How do you know?

HETTY: Because I saw him after my round last night, and he had just been talking to the Mobs and he told me.

DAVE: The idiot! And he's doing it this morning?

HETTY: Think so.

DAVE: But he ain't old enough – to ride, I mean. And they need a bike to do the run.

HETTY: They're thinking up something special for him.

ABE: That's right.

DAVE: You saw them an' all?

ABE: Er – yeah! He was with that Archie in the playground last night when I was going home.

DAVE: And you talked to them an' all?

ABE: Yeah . . . we had a few words!

DAVE: How nice! I hope you enjoyed yourself.

ABE: I wouldn't say that exactly.

DAVE: Make me sick, them Mobs.

ABE: I think I could say the same.

HETTY: Anyway – all that doesn't help us to find the money, does it?

DAVE: I'm not so sure. When I got to Gran's, she said that she thought I'd been in earlier. That's what worried me straight away, or I might just have thought one of you had got it and not bothered. But she heard someone come into the flat and heard them in the living room. About eight she thought it was. She didn't think it was me, but by the time she got up to look, whoever it was had gone.

ABE: Do you mean Slim might have pinched it?

DAVE: Why not! He was the only one who knew we keep the money on Fridays. He was the only other one of us who would know Gran's flat and that she'd be in bed at that time.

HETTY: But why would he want it?

DAVE: Cos if he's trying to get into the Mobs he's got to have a bike. Everybody knows that.

ABE: Well?

DAVE: Think it out, dumb-head! Slim hasn't been working here for more than six months. He only gets eighteen bob a week, and he smokes like a burning pile of dry leaves.

ABE: So where's the money coming from?

DAVE: Exactly.

HETTY: I don't think he'd do it though.

DAVE: What's more, now I come to think of it, he was asking about the money and whether we was taking it to Gran's, wasn't he? In the playground, last night.

ABE: Yeah – he was, Het.

HETTY: So what! I still don't think it would be him, that's all. I know he's pretty horrid, but I don't think he'd steal the paper money and I'm sure he wouldn't take it from your Gran's.

DAVE: He might if he wants a bike enough.

ABE: Yeah, Dave's right – if he wants a bike enough, he might do something as bad as that.

HETTY: Why not try the police first, Dave. There'll only be trouble and they'd be much quicker.

DAVE: Har-har! Yeah – they'd find it. And then what? Whoever had done it would get a ticking off from some doddering old Magistrate. (*Mimicking.*) You've been a very naughty boy to steal this money and I hope you won't do it again. I sentence you to one year's probation. (*Himself again.*) No fear – when I find out who's got that money, I'll deal with him myself.

HETTY: It'll only cause trouble, honest, Dave.

DAVE: Look – are you coming or not?

HETTY: I'm coming, but only to try and keep you from being pig-headed.

DAVE: Drip! Come on, Abe.

ABE: I'm right behind you, Dave.

Exit DAVE, ABRAHAM *and* HETTY.

SCENE THREE

The playground.

We hear SLIM *shouting as he runs to the playground. He enters, breathless and shouting: he is a frantic, desperate figure.*

SLIM: Dobber! Archie! Dobber! Dobber!

There is the roar of approaching motor bikes. They stop outside the playground. The MOBS *enter.* SLIM *calms down when he hears the bikes. The* MOBS *group round him, silent, menacing, savouring the coming chicken run.*

DOBBER: Ready, kid?

SLIM: I'm ready.

DOBBER: Now, kid, if you was the right age and could ride a machine on the road, you'd have a proper run, see? But as you can't, we've thought up a little chicken run specially for you.

SLIM: What is it?

DOBBER: You'll see. You got to know the rules first. Simple. Whatever happens you got to swear nothing goes any further. If anybody gets hurt – you know what I mean? – there's no screaming home to mummy, or telling the coppers, or anything like that – O.K.?

SLIM: O.K.

DOBBER: Now the important bit. Whatever happens to you, you haven't got to give up, or cry off, or nothing like that because if you do that's . . .

THE MOBS (*shouting*): *CHICKEN!*

DOBBER: You're scared and no use for the Mobs. Right?

SLIM: And if I stick it?

DOBBER: If you stick it, you're O.K., and in the Mobs, even if you are still in your nappies! Set it up, Queenie.

QUEENIE *takes two candles and sets them up on one of the boxes. They are placed about two feet apart. She lights them, holds the flaming match up, walks towards* SLIM, *blows the match out close to his face, grins at him, and returns to her first position.*

DOBBER: Now, watch, kid. Mutie, here.

MUTE *and* DOBBER *pace to the boxes, where the candles are burning. The scene begins to take on the look of a ritual, though clearly a ritual the* MOBS *relish. It has, however, a rhythm, a terrible inevitability about it.* MUTE *and* DOBBER *place themselves either side of the box, the*

*candles between them. They clasp their right hands to-
gether, place their elbows between the candles and begin
to test each other's strength. It is at once clear that which-
ever one loses will have his hand forced by the other into
the candle flame, which lies in the way of the fist if it is
forced down. At first,* MUTE *gets the advantage, but* DOB-
BER *soon begins the game in earnest, and* MUTE's *fist
is forced into the flame. He winces and tenses, but makes
little sound other than the forced breaths the pain causes.
He reacts away when* DOBBER *releases his hand, rubs the
back of his fist, then walks with assumed lightness to* SLIM,
shows him the fist, laughs, and walks away.

DOBBER: Get the idea, kid?

SLIM *nods, unable to speak.*

DOBBER: Want to go through with it?

SLIM *looks at* MUTE, *uncertain, but nods again.*

DOBBER: All righty. Bird – the straws.

BIRD *puts four straws into* DOBBER's *hand.*

DOBBER: Now, kid. Bird's got these straws, see. And
some are longer than others. She's going to take them
to Mute, and Archie, and Queenie, and me. We'll
draw. The one with the longest is the one you take
on. Right?

SLIM: Right.

DOBBER, ARCHIE, QUEENIE *and* MUTE *line up,
facing out.* SLIM *goes to one side, watching anxiously.*
BIRD *takes the straws from* DOBBER *and walks round
to the end of the line. As she passes* SLIM *she shows him
the straws, provocatively. Each of the four* MOBS *in turn
takes a straw, putting it out of sight behind his back as it
is drawn out of* BIRD's *hand. When all have drawn,* BIRD
walks away, turns, and gives the order to show.

BIRD: Show!

The four MOBS *show their straws.* DOBBER'S *is the longest. He looks along the line, smiling, then approaches* SLIM.

DOBBER: Looks like you're stuck with me, kid. So let's see you. (*He stubs his straw against* SLIM'S *chest and goes to the boxes.* SLIM *follows him.*)

DOBBER: Bird – you be umpire. See fair play! (*He kisses her.* DOBBER *and* SLIM *take up their positions.*)

BIRD: Fat chance he has anyway agin you. But you can get your elbow in for a start. The kid hasn't any chance at all with it stuck out there.

DOBBER: Ho-ho! Tough umpire-stuff, eh?

BIRD: Better. Both ready? After three you're on your own. One . . . two . . . three.

DOBBER and SLIM *take the strain. The others crane forward to see. There is little shouting at first, rather a cool sadistic enjoyment of the contest, but when* SLIM *begins to force* DOBBER'S *hand towards the candle, enthusiasm breaks and shouting begins.*

HETTY, DAVE *and* ABRAHAM *push their way on to the scene. Only* ARCHIE *tries to prevent them, but interest in the contest for both him and* DAVE *is too strong to allow much of a scuffle. They watch as* SLIM, *after a first taste of success, has his hand forced slowly back towards the candle. The* MOBS *shout louder and louder encouragement, but* DOBBER *is much the stronger boy, and* SLIM'S *hand is pushed slowly towards the candle. As it gets close* SLIM *begins to cry out and at once the others stop shouting and freeze: they watch the end with a cold lack of sympathy.*

SLIM: No! . . . No! . . . Please, no! Let go, please let go.

As DOBBER *holds the fist in the flame,* SLIM *screams*

out and sinks to his knees. DOBBER *pulls* SLIM *to his feet, climbs on to the box, holding* SLIM, *who is almost dangling from his arm, and throws him twisting to the ground.* DOBBER *kicks the candle off the box, at* SLIM'S *grovelling body, where he is whimpering, curled in a knot like a hedgehog protecting itself from attack.*

DOBBER: Chicken!

HETTY: That was a rotten, sick thing to do!

DOBBER (*dropping to the ground in front of* HETTY): What's it to you?

HETTY (*storming at him*): You put his hand into that flame deliberately, even when he was shouting not to. Calling *him* chicken! The kettle calling the pot black. Try someone your own size and then see how big and brave you are – you great bear!

DOBBER (*delighted*): Fire-ee! You Slim's little bit, are you?

> HETTY *glares at him with rage a moment, then slaps him sharply across the face. The* BIRD *springs at her.*

BIRD: Why, you little bitch!

> DOBBER *grabs* BIRD *as she passes him and pulls her to him.*

DOBBER: Jealous?

HETTY (*going to* SLIM): Are you all right, Slim?

SLIM: Leave me be.

HETTY: Let's see your hand.

SLIM (*stumbling from her*): Go drown yourself.

DAVE: That's what you get for not minding your own business. He's not through yet anyway.

HETTY: Leave him, Dave. You can't do anything now. Not after all this.

DAVE: He's got it coming – it's his own fault.

HETTY: Not now, Dave. Have some feelings.

DAVE: Feelings! What about him having some feelings about pinching the money from my Gran's?

HETTY: But you don't know he took it yet. He's in no state . . .

DAVE: Whose fault that? He wanted to do the chicken run, didn't he? He's only himself to blame for what's happened. You don't understand.

HETTY: *I* don't understand! I'll tell you what I understand and you don't. If you start on Slim now about that money you're as bad as that gorilla over there – just as bad.

DOBBER: Look, kid – what's all this about money and pinching?

DAVE: It's nothing to do with you.

HETTY: Nothing to do with him! The great baboon. If it hadn't been for him and his morons, none of this would have happened. (*To* DOBBER.) I'll tell you what he *thinks* has happened. He *thinks* Slim has stolen forty-two quid from his Gran's flat.

DOBBER: He's what!

SLIM: I haven't been near his Gran's. What would I want to pinch forty-two quid for anyway?

DAVE: You want to be in this lot, don't you? Well to do that you have to have a bike, and to have a bike you have to have money. You haven't enough money to buy your next packet of fags never mind a motor bike. Does that spell it out for you?

SLIM (*desperate, frightened, frustrated and hurt*): It's not me, I tell you. Why can't you leave me alone! I've had enough. I'm going.

SLIM *thrusts his way between them as they crowd round*

him. DAVE *is not prepared to let him go and runs to block his exit.* DOBBER *sees the possibility of more fun and blocks his other way. The others scatter about the playground, hemming him in.*

SLIM (*confronting* DAVE *again*): Get out of my way, or I'll drop you.

DAVE: You ain't going 'till you've told us where you were this morning and who can clear you.

SLIM: Look, I'm warning you, I've had enough. Get out of my way, or I'll drop you, honest I will.

DAVE: Drop me! After the little show you just put up I'd say you couldn't drop a brick off a roof.

SLIM *is beside himself, provoked beyond endurance, an animal trapped on all sides.*

The MOBS *watch silent and enjoying the turn of events.* HETTY *holds* ABRAHAM *partly to protect him and partly to hold him back from rushing to* DAVE'S *assistance.*

SLIM *at last tries to make a way out. He is prevented by* DOBBER, *and turning, finds the climbing ladder near him. He grabs it desperately and finds a loose bar. He pulls it free. Holding it like a two-handed sword, he makes for* DAVE.

SLIM: Now – get out of my way.

DOBBER: Watch it, kid – he'll have yer.

DAVE *holds his ground, until at last* SLIM *jabs at him with the rod.* DAVE *side-steps, grabs the other end of the rod and with a great sweep of his body, swings* SLIM *so that he crashes against the proscenium arch, leaving go of the rod.*

The MOBS *cheer.* DAVE, *infected by his success, strolls away from* SLIM, *holding the bar above his head in victory. But* SLIM, *recovering, rushes to him, turns back to back*

with DAVE, *takes the bar and pulls it down, bending for-*
ward, so that DAVE *is flung in a great somersault over his*
head, landing heavily and leaving the bar in SLIM'S *hands.*

WILF, *on top of the climbing ladder, seeing which way*
things are going, has ripped another piece of rod from the
ladder, and as DAVE *jumps to his feet to defend himself*
against SLIM *calls* 'Here, kid' *and throws the bar to*
DAVE, *who receives it only just in time to defend himself*
against SLIM'S *first chopping thrust at his head.*

A furious battle ensues, SLIM *working out of himself*
all the pent-up misery that is in him, DAVE *desperately*
defending himself against the attack, playing always a de-
fender's role. It is an odd mixture of sword fighting, staff
fighting and wrestling, and carries the two boys round the
playground, the others keeping a safe distance, but yelling
their encouragement, their loyalties now entirely with
DAVE. *At last the battle takes* DAVE *and* SLIM *scampering*
up the ladder, the one for extra defence, the other forced to
follow. It is difficult on top of the ladder to maintain balance
and they are edging cautiously towards each other, when
GRAN *enters, distraught and breathless. Seeing the two boys*
on the ladder she cries out.

GRAN: Davie!

The cry distracts DAVE *just at the moment when* SLIM
swings his rod. The blow knocks DAVE *screaming to the*
ground, where he rolls in pain holding his foot. The others
crowd round him, except SLIM, *who stands watching from*
the top of the ladder shocked by what has happened, his
fury evaporated.

GRAN: Don't touch him!

GRAN *bends over* DAVE, *and inspects his leg.*

GRAN: All right, David. It's all right. You've only hurt

ϸ

it bad. Nothing broke, I think. Lift him on to them boxes.

DOBBER *and* TICH *lift* DAVID *on to the boxes.* DOBBER *supports him from behind.*

HETTY: Is he all right, Gran?

ABE: All right, Dave?

GRAN: It's only a sprain, I think. But we'd best be careful. Whatever were you doing, you silly lad?

DOBBER: All right, kid?

DAVE: I'm O.K. Honest. Ankle hurts bad, that's all. What did you shout for, Gran?

GRAN: It was the shock, you see. Seeing you up there like that. You do play some daft games, I must say. Dangerous that one is. And I was all of a tiz about the money. Dear, me, I've nearly forgotten what I came for. It's this. (*She takes a yellow scarf from her pocket.*) I found it in the flat this morning after you'd gone. It's not mine, son.

HETTY: Why is it important, Gran?

GRAN: It was in the flat, Hetty, love. Didn't realize it was there this morning when Dave come. It's not mine so it must have been dropped by whoever come in and took the money.

DAVE (*taking the scarf and looking at it*): Well it ain't mine.

The significance of the scarf is not lost on the MOBS. *When they see it, they begin to square-up.* ARCHIE *realizes the scarf is his.* DOBBER *is staring straight at him.* MUTE *edges behind* ARCHIE. *Suddenly there is a cry from* DAVE *as* DOBBER *lets him go, to be caught by* TICH. DOBBER *makes for* ARCHIE *who is taken from behind by* MUTE. *As* DOBBER *comes to them,* MUTE *throws* ARCHIE *to him.* DOBBER *catches* ARCHIE *by the arms and bends them up behind* ARCHIE'S *back, bending him forward.*

DOBBER: Well, well, Archie, old lad. Lost anything, have you?

ARCHIE: Chuck it, will you!

DOBBER (*applying more pressure*): Don't come that with me, Archie. Have you lost anything?

ARCHIE: No! (*Dobber applies more pressure until* ARCHIE *can take no more.*) O.K. It's mine. It's mine. Leave off.

DOBBER *throws* ARCHIE *back to* MUTE *and stands away from them.*

DOBBER: Turn him out, Wilf.

WILF *crosses to* ARCHIE *and rips open his leathers. He pulls him forward by his shirt.* MUTE *pulls the jacket from* ARCHIE *and throws it to* DOBBER. WILF *passes* ARCHIE *back to* MUTE *and searches* ARCHIE.

WILF (*moving away*): Nothing!

DOBBER *holds out* ARCHIE'S *jacket, slowly unzips a side pocket, and takes from it the money bag. He holds it out to* GRAN.

DOBBER: This what you looking for, Missus?

GRAN: Yes, but . . . This is all more than I can take.

GRAN *staggers and leans against the boxes.* HETTY *supports her.* ABRAHAM *takes the bag from* DOBBER.

DAVE: How did Archie know about it? Nobody but the newskids knew.

DOBBER: Maybe he's just the burgling sort.

SLIM (*who has watched it all from where he is sitting on top of the ladder*): I told him.

DOBBER: *You* told him! What for?

SLIM: He was asking about the news round, and how it worked. He said he had to know about things like that so the Mobs would know I was O.K. Said there was no secrets in the Mobs.

DOBBER (*confronting* ARCHIE): Well, well, Archie. That was very conscientious of you. No secrets! Well here's a little secret you can share with us, mate. You're out. That's it for you, Archie. You're on your own.

ARCHIE (*shaking loose from* MUTE): So what! You think that worries me? You think being kicked out of this lot worries me? God – honestly! You're a set of kids having a game. A bunch of thick-heads playing at being big. You're all brawn and no brain. And one day you'll be skinfuls of fat!

DOBBER: You reckon? Well I'll tell you something, Archie. We aren't done with you. Not by no means. You aren't through yet. Letting the coppers get you is too nice a fate altogether. You might have give that old woman her money back – with our help, of course! – but there's some things you still got to pay for, mate. You owe us one or two things, Archie. (MUTE *and* WILF *have come behind* ARCHIE.) And we're gonna squeeze you dry. We're gonna hang you up and drain it out of you drop by drop. (*He pushes* ARCHIE *into* MUTE *and* WILF, *who hold him.*)

ARCHIE (*struggling*): Let me go!

DOBBER: Hard to get in – easy to get out. But on the way out you have some debts to pay. Take him to the shack.

ARCHIE *is taken out, struggling, by* MUTE *and* WILF.

DOBBER: Tich – take that Dave kid and give him a free ride on your machine to the quack-man.

TICH *lifts* DAVE *off the boxes and carries him off.*

GRAN: You'll never do it. Wouldn't it be best to get an ambulance?

DAVE: I'm all right, Gran. Stop worrying. I'll manage. Anyway, it'll be worth it, just to get a ride on his bike!

Exit TICH *carrying* DAVE.

GRAN: I'm off home. I'm feeling all upset.

HETTY: I'll come with you, Gran.

GRAN (*walking with difficulty and breathing heavily*): That's very kind of you, Hetty. I hope they don't find anything wrong with Dave's foot. But I really don't feel I can go all the way to the doctor's, I'm right done in . . .

Exit GRAN *and* HETTY, *helping her.* ABRAHAM *follows.* DOBBER *signals the other* MOBS *to leave him. Exit* QUEENIE *and the* BIRD.

DOBBER *turns and looks up at* SLIM *who is sitting dejected on the climbing ladder.*

DOBBER: That was a good show you put up with that kid, Slim.

Pause. SLIM *doesn't answer, and is motionless.*

DOBBER: Good as a chicken run. (SLIM *remains silent and unmoving.*) I know how you feel, kid. Tell you what. We'll count that fight as your run – O.K.? (*He holds up Archie's jacket.*) Here – take that crumb's coat. It's yours. You're a Mob.

DOBBER *waits a moment, holding up the coat. When* SLIM *shows no sign of response,* DOBBER *turns away, stops by the boxes, and lays the coat on them. He looks back at* SLIM *then exits.*

The noise of motor bikes starting and roaring off. The sound seems to drag SLIM *from his self-absorbtion. He looks off, as though at the departing bikes. Then slowly, as the noise goes into the distance, he climbs down from the ladder, still carrying the rod he fought with. He comes to the boxes, staring at the jacket laid across them. Then as the noise of the bikes disappears, he raises the rod slowly and deliberately and finally swings it down with all his strength on to the jacket. The scene fades out.*

SCENE FOUR

The bench by the canal.
MEGEN, *in her waterproofs, sits dejectedly watching her float out on the canal. The empty packet of Maltesers is in her hands.* TROUT *is prepaing a new cast.*

MEGEN (*after a pause full of sighs*): The Maltesers is finished.
   Pause.
MEGEN: When are we going back, Trout?
TROUT: Back? We've only been here a couple of hours.
MEGEN: Feels like we've been here all day.
TROUT: Sometimes I stay all day.
MEGEN: You do!
TROUT: You'll soon get used to it – when you've caught a fish or two.
MEGEN: Doubt if I'll survive that long.
TROUT: Just one good fish – see then. Here, hold this for me. (*He hands her a small white thing.*)
   MEGEN *holds out her hand without looking. When* TROUT *drops the maggot into her hand, she screams, jumps up, throwing the maggot away.*
TROUT (*on his knees searching*): What d'you do that for? Just a maggot. Good fat 'un too.

MEGEN: Oo – I can't stand them, Trout, honest I can't. Squiggly, squirmy things. And they smell too.

TROUT (*with relish*): Better than when they turn into great blue-bottles. I kept some maggots once, and they were all in a tin. And I opened the tin in our kitchen and all these big fat blue-bottles swarmed out. *Lovely!*

MEGEN (*sitting again*): Oo – do hush, Trout. I'm feeling ill.

They settle again. MEGEN *looks off, at her float. Her eyes light up.*

MEGEN: My little float's gone.

TROUT: You mean under? Well, strike, woman. Strike!

MEGEN *snatches up her rod and strikes. The rod bends and kicks heavily.* MEGEN *tries to wind in, and is pulled slowly towards the water.*

TROUT: You've got something! Something big! Wind in! Wind in! (*Shouting now.*) Wind in!

MEGEN: I am winding in. Help me, Trout. Help!

TROUT: I *am* helping! WIND IN!

MEGEN *disappears off, screaming as she goes.* TROUT *scampers about as though following her progress along the bankside.*

TROUT: Keep winding, Meg. Don't let the line slack. Steady, Meg, steady, the bank's slippery there. Steady . . . Meg!

There is a scream from MEGEN, *and* TROUT *dives off after her. The shouting goes on, amidst splashes and water sounds.*

Enter MEGEN *beaming, hatless, rodless, soaked to the skin, but triumphantly carrying a huge fish.* TROUT *follows also soaked. They stop, facing each other by the bench.* MEGEN *holds the fish like a small child.*

TROUT: You've done it! Done it! That's bigger than I've had for months. Than I've ever had.

MEGEN: Trout! Wasn't it super! Super, Trout! Oh – Trout, our first fish!

TROUT: Eh? Oh – yeah!

MEGEN: And you dived in after me.

TROUT: Yeah – well you might have lost the fish if I hadn't.

MEGEN: And I might have drowned.

TROUT: Well . . . yeah . . . there is that about it.

MEGEN: That was ever so brave of you, Trout.

TROUT: It was?

MEGEN: I'll never complain about your maggots again, Trout.

TROUT: You won't?

MEGEN: No – though I do hope we don't have to dive in every time.

TROUT: It doesn't happen every time, Meg.

MEGEN: I'm so glad.

They are gawping at one another.

TROUT: Here – let's go and tell the others.

MEGEN: Oo – yes. They'll never believe it.

They gather their things and exit.

SCENE FIVE

LES'S *shop.*

LES *is sorting papers.* ABRAHAM *is sitting on the counter head in hands.* HETTY *is sitting on a chair, dejected.*

MEGEN *and* TROUT *enter, still wet but overjoyed by their success by the canal.*

TROUT: You'll never believe it, you lot. Megen's caught a whacking great fish. Look!

MEGEN: Nearly drowned getting it, I did. But Trout saved me. He's that brave!

HETTY: Megen, Trout. Something's happened.

TROUT: That's what I'm telling you. Look – Meg caught it.

LES: Shut up, Trout. Hetty's being serious.

TROUT: She is an' all. Let me guess. From the length of your faces I'd say you'd had your wages stopped.

MEGEN: Oh – don't say that, Trout! Think about my transistor.

ABE: Dave's sprained his ankle. It's bad.

TROUT: Sprained his ankle. How?

ABE: Fell off that climbing ladder in the playground.

HETTY: He had a fight with Slim Mackee.

MEGEN: Fighting Slim Mackee! Thought something like that would happen in the end.

TROUT: I hope he give him what for, that's all.

MEGEN: What started it, Het?

HETTY: Dave thought Slim had stolen the paper money from Gran's flat.

TROUT: Crikey!

MEGEN: Oo – I knew it would go back in the end!

ABE: It's all right. We've got the money back.

HETTY: That Archie Mickloe had pinched it. There was an awful fight, Meg.

MEGEN: Don't you worry about Dave's leg, Het, he'll be all right after a bit.

Enter DAVE, *his leg heavily bandaged, and using walking sticks.*

LES (*going to him*): You shouldn't have come to the shop, Dave.

ABE: We could have coped.

HETTY: Are you all right, Dave?

DAVE: I'm all right, honest. Stop fussing, will you!

LES: But you can't do a round like that, Dave. Not with your leg like that.

DAVE: I know, Les. But I can help in the shop – put the papers up and do a bit of serving behind the counter, can't I?

LES: Well, I dunno . . .

DAVE: I don't want to stay at home, Les.

LES: Well, all right. Just so long as you don't stand around on that foot too long.

DAVE: I won't, honest.

LES (*to Trout and Megen*): Look, you two, you'd better hop off home and get changed. You look like drowned rats as you are. There's nowt you can do here until rounds time. You're better off out of the way.

TROUT: Just off, Les.

DAVE: Been swimming, have you?

TROUT: Megen caught a whacking great fish, Dave.

DAVE: Great!

MEGEN: Nearly drowned getting it, I did. But Trout saved me – he's that brave!

DAVE: Looks as though you're hooked, Trout!

TROUT (*not comprehending at first*): Hooked? How d'you mean? Oh! (*He laughs.*)

MEGEN: Sorry to hear about your ankle, Dave.

TROUT: Me too, Dave.

DAVE: Thanks, both of you.

TROUT: Hope you gave that Slim what for!

DAVE: I did my best, Trout.

TROUT: Yeah . . . well, see yer, Dave.

MEGEN: 'Bye, Davie.

Exit MEGEN *and* TROUT.

LES: Look, Dave, I'm just going upstairs to change, so's I can have me tea and do your round.

ABE: You do Dave's round?

LES: Why not?

ABE: You haven't done a round for years. You'll probably collapse from exhaustion!

LES: What d'you mean! I'm as fit as I ever was. Anyway, it'll make a change. Just hang on, will you, Dave?

DAVE: Leave it to me, Les.

Exit LES.

DAVE and HETTY *go behind the counter and begin sorting. Now the three are together again, an uneasy, almost embarrassed silence settles between them.* ABRAHAM *is uneasy and shuffles.* HETTY *and* DAVE *avoid each other's eyes. Then both look at each other at once.*

DAVE (*a little raw*): So I was wrong.

They go on looking at each other. ABRAHAM *avoids them.* HETTY *remains silent.* DAVE *shrugs.*

DAVE (*softening*): I'm sorry, Hetty.

HETTY (*smiling*): Forget it!

Pause. Enter SLIM. *He is brisk, holding himself, steeled against other people, their comments, and himself. But there is a determination in his words we've not heard before.*

ABE (*antagonistic*): What do you want?

DAVE: Shut up, Abe.

SLIM: I was wanting to see Les.

DAVE: He's upstairs having his tea. You're too early for your papers.

SLIM: I wanted to tell him that I'm packing in my round. I'll work until the end of a week, but after that I'm quitting.

ABE: Good!

DAVE: I know how you feel, Slim, and you can finish now if you like. We can manage: there's somebody waiting for your round so we can set him on straight away.

SLIM: Yeah – just as you like.

HETTY: Don't give up the round just because of what's happened, Slim.

SLIM: I'm not.

ABE: What *are* you chucking it for, then? You're running, aren't you? Running, cos you chickened.

SLIM: All right, so I chickened. But they won't catch me like that again. Nobody will ever get me like the Mobs did, not again. Another month at school, then I'll be out of it. I'll have my own money, and me own place, and I'll be out of all this. I don't care what you think and I don't care what you do, because nobody can hurt me any more, not any of you.

HETTY: We don't want to hurt you, Slim.

SLIM: That's as maybe. But I ain't taking any chances. Nobody is ever going to touch me again. Not anybody.

ABE: What if you can't stop them, what then?

SLIM: I don't care. They can do what they like. You can get hurt so much it doesn't hurt any more, you go numb and it's just something you've got to put up with. But they won't get the chance, because they won't get close enough to try.

DAVE: So you're packing in your news round, and saving for your bike and all that?

SLIM: Yeah.

DAVE: But that's giving up.

SLIM: Is it?

DAVE: It wouldn't do for me.

ABE: Nor me. I don't scare that easy.

SLIM: I ain't frightened, kid. For the first time in my life, I ain't frightened. (*Pause.*) See yer.

    Exit SLIM.

ABE: Well, I'm glad he's gone. Good riddance, I say.

HETTY: Somehow, I think we'll miss him.

ABE: You might, I won't.

DAVE (*holding an empty newsbag out to* ABE): Here, hold this, will you.

ABE: Yeah – and what's this about somebody waiting for a round? I haven't heard Les talking about anybody waiting for one. He's always saying he can't get new kids.

DAVE: There just happens to be someone who's been waiting for weeks. Right, Hetty?

HETTY: For weeks.

ABE: Who, Dave?

    DAVE *and* HETTY *say nothing, just look at each other and then at* ABE *in a steady stare, smiling.*

ABE (*understanding dawning*): You mean . . . you mean . . . I can have Slim's old round?

DAVE: What else?

ABE: Honest, Dave? What'll Les say?

DAVE: He'll say yes, you'll see.

ABE (*overjoyed*): Crikey, Dave, thanks.

DAVE: Well, go on. There's too much lazing around in this shop. What do you think you're on – Daddy's yacht? Get a move on. Get your tea or you'll be late for your round.

ABE: Yeah, yeah, Dave. See yer.

DAVE: And, Abe?

ABE (*turning back*): Yeah?

DAVE: Beware of the dog!

    Exit ABE.

HETTY: I'd better be off home too, Dave.

DAVE: Yeah.

HETTY: I'm glad you came in the shop this afternoon, Dave.

DAVE: Me too.

HETTY: It's always best just to carry on as though everything was the same as ever.

DAVE: Yeah, I suppose so. (*Pause.*) Yet . . . nothing will ever be quite the same again, will it, Hetty?

HETTY: No – I suppose not. (*Pause.*) See yer, Dave.

DAVE: See you, Hetty.

    Exit HETTY.

    DAVID *sorts papers, slowly at first, but gaining in determination as the scene fades.*

THE END